Another Fawcett Crest Book
by James Melville:

THE WAGES OF ZEN

A SORT OF SAMURAI

James Melville

FAWCETT CREST • NEW YORK

A Fawcett Crest Book
Published by Ballantine Books
Copyright © 1981 by James Melville

Library of Congress Catalog Card Number: 81-16750

ISBN 0-449-20821-4

This edition published by arrangement with St. Martin's Press

Manufactured in the United States of America

First Ballantine Books Edition: December 1985

To the one who opened the door

THE CHARACTERS IN THE STORY

Tetsuo OTANI	Superintendent, Hyogo Prefectural Police
Hanae OTANI	His wife
Akiko SHIMIZU	Their daughter
Akira SHIMIZU	Their son-in-law
Kazuo SHIMIZU	Their grandson
Jiro KIMURA	
"Ninja" NOGUCHI	Police Inspectors
Masao SAKAMOTO	
Yasuo TOMITA	Otani's driver
Kenichi MIGISHIMA	Police constable
Tadashi HORIGUCHI	Retired professor
DANGORO XIII	Puppeteer
Baron Bunsho MAEDA	Businessman
Richard LIEBERMANN	Businessman
Irmgard LIEBERMANN	His wife
Ilse FISCHER	His secretary
Hiroshi ODA	A student

AUTHOR'S NOTE

Hyogo is a real prefecture, and it has a police force. It should be emphasised therefore that all the characters in this story are wholly fictitious and bear no relation to any actual person, living or dead.

やはり侍

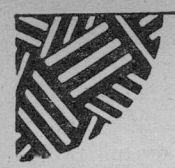

Chapter 1

HANAE LOOKED ROUND QUICKLY TO MAKE SURE THAT nobody was about, then tried again. This time she managed to grasp her ankles firmly enough to be able to peer for a moment upside down between her legs at the narrow promontory on the coast of the Japan Sea known as the Bridge of Heaven. "Well, I *suppose* I can understand why they say so," she gasped in a strangulated voice. Superintendent Tetsuo Otani of Hyogo Prefectural Police looked down in silence at the small, contorted figure of his wife. Then he took her hand as she righted herself, her face flushed and the strands of glossy black hair out of place making her look a good deal younger than her years.

She looked up at him contentedly, unintimidated by what seemed to most people to be the grim and forbidding set of his features. Otani had never played poker in his life, but he might have made a fortune at the game if he had tried. Even today, on a warm and sunny late April afternoon, and dressed casually in a short-sleeved red and white checked sports shirt, cotton trousers and simple leather sandals, he looked like a man of authority.

For a man in his early fifties he was in pretty good shape: not tall even among Japanese of his own generation, he was

1

dwarfed by many of the beefy young policemen who held him in awe at Prefectural Headquarters in Kobe. His skin was distinctly swarthy, and when contrasting it with her own creamy whiteness Hanae would sometimes tease him a little. Not too much: just enough to tempt him to direct at her the murderous scowl he did as well as any *kabuki* actor and which never failed to make her ache with laughter.

"You sound doubtful," he said after a while, still holding Hanae's hand and looking out at the twisted pines which clung improbably to the weathered grey-blue boulders of the Bridge. "You should have more respect for the place where the gods decided to make a start on Japan. *Ama-no-hashidate* . . . it's a fine sounding name."

Hanae nodded. "Mmmm, it is. But I still can't quite see why you have to look at it upside down."

"Because it's a bridge to *heaven*, and heaven is up, not down, you ignorant and undeserving slut." Otani looked at her sternly as he deliberately used the old-fashioned derogatory word for one's own wife, and Hanae joined in the game.

"You may have one or two of those tucked away somewhere," she said in a hoity-toity accent of the kind affected by the girls who stand at the foot of the escalators in department stores, white-gloved and immaculate, "but speaking as your *honourable consort*, I am bound to say that it doesn't look much like a bridge to me. And it's not very respectful to the gods for it to be called the *third* most beautiful place in Japan." She paused, struck by the thought. "Where are the first and second?" The question was put in her normal voice, and made Otani chuckle.

"I haven't the slightest idea," he admitted. "The Grand Shrine at Ise? The Imperial Palace? Miyajima? Anyway, I'm enjoying myself. I haven't been here since my father brought me when I was a little boy. Imagine what it will be like in a week or so." They both stood quietly for a moment, taking in the almost deserted coastline, and watching a small fishing-boat puttering towards the quay.

"It was lovely to come away just *before* Golden Week," Hanae agreed. "It's a shame that most people have to go away at the same time, but what can you expect, with three

2

public holidays in the same week? Come, we'd better be getting back to the inn.'' She squeezed Otani's hand quickly before releasing it for the sake of propriety as they turned and headed for the village with its scatter of inns, houses and souvenir-shops.

''A mixture of good fortune and judgement, as far as I'm concerned,'' said Otani. ''When I was agreeing the duty roster for Golden Week I thought it would be a lot more sensible to take a week off now and then have a quiet time in the office into the bargain instead of getting on to crowded trains and buses with everybody else in Japan.''

''Where's Kimura-san going?'' asked Hanae.

Otani's mouth twitched. ''Inspector Kimura was rather cagey when I enquired, but eventually confessed that he is proposing to take a package holiday in Taiwan. It's called the Bachelor's Romance Special in the travel brochure, but Ninja Noguchi has another name for it.''

Hanae tut-tutted unconvincingly. Jiro Kimura's indefatigable lechery was no doubt deplorable, but she had a very soft spot for him all the same. She changed the subject. ''How long will it take us to get to Professor Horiguchi's house?'' she asked.

''No more than twenty minutes or so by taxi,'' said Otani, glancing at an appetizing display of dried squid outside the open-fronted shop they were passing. ''It's just the other side of Miyazu, and that's hardly any distance. It will be pleasant to see the old gentleman again. The only one of Father's close colleagues still living. I remember when I was a boy he used to come to the house quite often.''

They arrived at the entrance to the simple wooden buildings of their inn. The Kissei-Ro was a comfortable old place of the kind Otani always sought out where possible, and he shouted ''We're back!'' cheerfully as he kicked off his sandals and stepped up on to the polished wooden step and the worn but clean tatami mats of the entrance. The flower arrangement in a flat earthenware dish in the *tokonoma* alcove was rather clumsy and unsophisticated, like the fresh-faced country girl who rushed from the kitchen regions, the sleeves of her dark blue cotton kimono held back from her plump arms by the red tapes of her apron.

She sank to her knees with awkward grace and welcomed the guests on their return, as she would with equal sincerity whether they came back twice or twenty times during the day. Hanae lingered for a minute or two to discuss the menu for their evening meal while Otani shuffled into a pair of the floppy backless slippers lined up at the beginning of the wooden corridor and made his way to their room, passing a small and not particularly elegant side garden in which an old man was watering a stone lantern.

The room they had been allotted was like the rest of the inn; comfortable, but homely and unpretentious. Eight mats was a very fair size, roughly twelve feet square, but a sense of much greater space was achieved by the fact that the sliding wood and paper shoji screens at the outer side opened on to another larger garden. The early afternoon sunshine flooded in, giving a golden glow to the tatami mats and making the old lacquer table, with its massively curved but stubby eight-inch legs, gleam dully.

Otani plonked himself down at the table appreciatively, the material of the flat cushion on which he sat warm to his backside, and waited for Hanae to appear. When she did, she was followed by the maid, bringing damp hot towels and green tea. They mopped their faces, Otani vigorously and Hanae delicately, and sipped the tea in peaceful silence.

Then Hanae stood up and surveyed her husband. "Will I do as I am?" she enquired.

Otani looked up at her. She was wearing Western dress, a quiet green blouse and skirt, and he nodded at once. "You look fine," he said. "Better take a woollen thing to put on, though. It'll probably be cold in his house, even on a warm day like this. I shall have to change, of course."

"Even when you're on holiday?" Hanae was sympathetic.

"I think so," said Otani regretfully. "He is eighty-four after all. In his day he was a bit of a radical—I think he got into trouble with the police before the war for 'dangerous thoughts'. All the same, I think he'd be shocked if I were to

4

call on him dressed like this. Still, even in his time the younger professors were beginning to wear sports jackets and slacks, so that's what I'll put on. At least I won't look like a policeman. Did you order a taxi?''

Hanae nodded, and went to repair her make-up and do her hair, kneeling in front of the tiny dressing-table not much bigger than doll's house furniture. Otani rummaged in the big cupboard where their modest quantity of luggage was stored and began to change his clothes. There was plenty of time. Professor Horiguchi's letter, written in an old-fashioned but firm style of calligraphy with a proper brush, had expressed his delight on hearing that the son of his old colleague from Osaka University days would be staying near his retirement home with his wife, and had cordially invited them both to tea at four o'clock.

He must have heard the car pull up, because the front door of the big old house built of brick in the Western style opened as Hanae and Otani approached it and there he was on the step, upright and dapper in a pin-striped suit with a gold watch-chain across the waistcoat, hand outstretched and a broad smile on his face. Tadashi Horiguchi, Member of the Japan Academy, Honorary Fellow of the Royal Society of London and Emeritus Professor of Geology at Osaka National University, seemed to be in splendid form.

''You are most courteously punctual,'' he said as he pumped Otani's hand vigorously and then seized Hanae's, to her great confusion ''Now come along, come along into my study. No, no, please keep your shoes *on*. I live in the Western manner, you know.'' It was agony to both Hanae and Otani to obey this genial instruction, and it was only after he repeated it and they looked down at the Professor's gleaming black shoes that they brought themselves to step gingerly inside and walk over a richly patterned carpet to the study, wincing as they went.

''I learned to appreciate afternoon tea when I visited Balliol College in Oxford in the ninth year of Showa. That's getting on for forty-five years or so ago,'' the old gentleman continued as he led the way. ''And afternoon tea must *always* be taken at four o'clock, you know." He nodded his beautiful head of silver hair a few times as if in confirmation. "Now then, in you go."

The room was a revelation to Hanae, whose experience of Western-style living was restricted to occasional nights in hotels, meals in restaurants and the view of life in the West afforded by films and television, which hardly counted. She summoned up the self-discipline of her girlhood to prevent herself from gaping about her idiotically, and untied the silk *furoshiki* wrapper she was carrying. Their present was a simple one, consisting of a bottle of the best Kobe *sake*, but Professor Horiguchi accepted it as though it were a rare treasure.

"Well now, my dear lady—if I may so address you," he said after thanking them both effusively, "I wonder if you would be so kind as to be mother, as they say in England. My housekeeper has prepared everything, as you see . . . Twining's tea, which you no doubt drink at home, and there is milk or lemon; and a few morsels to eat. Now tell me, Otani-san, have you ever had a proper cucumber sandwich before?"

They sat down, and Professor Horiguchi watched happily as Hanae poured tea from a delicate pot, on tenterhooks lest she should spill so much as a single drop, and eventually they were all settled with their cups and plates. As she nibbled at the strange but by no means unpleasant cucumber sandwich and listened to the conversation, Hanae was at last able to adjust to the awareness of the real leather of the armchair in which she sat, the quiet ticking of a clock on a kind of shelf which projected above a place for a fire to burn, the walls lined with bookshelves, and a great many photographs in frames; some standing on pieces of heavy wooden furniture, others hung on the walls. It was, she eventually decided, a very pleasant room, although it was so odd.

Hanae became so absorbed in her reverie that she thought at first that she must be dreaming when she suddenly became aware of the question her husband was asking. "But what does it matter to a catfish anyway?" he demanded in a slightly mutinous manner as he reached for a piece of fruit cake from the plate on the table.

Professor Horiguchi nodded affably. "You mean, why

should an earthquake be of any concern to a creature which lives in the water? A good question, Otani-san. I see that although you did not elect to pursue an academic career, you have inherited a scientist's curiosity from your eminent father.'' He caught Hanae's eye and twinkled, and she hastily closed her mouth, which had been slightly open in her bewilderment. The old man beamed at her kindly, and took pity.

''You may have missed the first part of our little discussion, my dear madam,'' he said. ''Your husband was good enough to enquire whether I kept up my interest in earthquakes, and what I thought of the efforts being made here and there to predict their occurrence by observation of the behaviour of catfish.'' The power of the old man's personality was extraordinary, and its warmth embraced them both as he spoke. Hanae now sat spellbound, refilling their teacups almost mechanically when Professor Horiguchi pushed his own forward a fraction of an inch in mid-sentence with a delicate flicker of one bushy white eyebrow.

''There has always been a considerable folklore on this theme, you know. I have been amusing myself in my retirement by scribbling a few notes on the life of a very remarkable Englishman who lived in Yokohama back in the Meiji period. His name was Milne.'' The Professor pronounced it ''Mirrun''. ''Yes. 'Earthquake' Milne, he liked to be called, or sometimes 'Earthquake Johnny'. He came to Japan in the late nineteenth century like many European scholars. He was fascinated by our earthquakes, being a geologist, and they told him—quite wrongly as it happens—that they occur in Yokohama more frequently than anywhere else in the country.''

He sipped delicately at his tea, nodding his thanks to Hanae, then went on. ''So he set up the first seismograph in Japan at Yokohama—he earned his living as the Imperial Government's Inspector of Mines, by the way—and spent all his spare time recording tremors. Plenty of them, needless to say.'' Professor Horiguchi set down his cup and saucer with care and opened his bright black eyes wide, his hands on his thin knees. He leaned forward conspiratorially.

"But do you know what?" he enquired. Hanae and Otani shook their heads in silence, neither wishing to break the spell. *"He wasn't satisfied,"* crowed the old man delightedly. "No. This extraordinary fellow hired some labourers to rig up a sort of crane apparatus and got hold of an enormous cast iron ball which he could hoist up to the top and then drop to the ground from about ten metres or so. Boom!" Professor Horiguchi flung his arms exuberantly upwards and outwards. "Just to make the needle of his seismograph flicker! What a man!"

They all sat in silence for a time after that, with Hanae desperately avoiding Otani's eye. She was enchanted by the tale and the manner of its telling, but at the same time was possessed by a powerful urge to dissolve into giggles, most inappropriate for a matron in her forties. She felt quite cheated at not having had an opportunity to meet this delightful old man before.

The Professor meditated for a while, then resumed his story. "Doctor Milne left quite extensive notes which found their way to the University library, and a former student of mine who is now there has most kindly sent me photocopies. All in English, of course, though it is clear that our man acquired a more than serviceable command of Japanese . . . they did, in those days. Would you credit it that another Englishman was Professor of *Japanese* of all things in the Imperial University at that time? Chamberlain, his name was. From a naval family, I believe. You are a former Navy man, are you not, Otani-san?"

"Yes," said Otani quietly. "Right at the end of the war, I left senior high school and managed to get a temporary commission. Mainly through the influence of your old acquaintance Baron Maeda, I suppose. He was a captain then. That's why I never went to university." A chill seemed to fall on the room for a moment, and Otani smiled a twisted little smile. "I'm afraid your colleague my father never really forgave me, Horiguchi-sensei."

The old man nodded. "I know. Your father was a fine chemist, an honourable man— and distinctly pig-headed. He never could see that we needed men like you to replace the police who gave *us* such a bad time." He mused for a moment, then looked up perkily as another thought struck him.

"What is the Baron doing these days, by the way? We always thought of him as a young man, but I suppose he too must be retired by now. Do you see him at all?"

Hanae felt emboldened to join in. She was very fond of Bunsho Maeda, who had not only served as the formal go-between at their wedding even though it had in fact been arranged by a distant cousin but had been one of the principal mourners at the funeral of Otani's father.

"We're not supposed to call him 'Baron' now, sensei," she said shyly. "Just plain Maeda-san. I think he's very well. My husband sees him every week at the Rotary Club."

Otani nodded and smiled. "Well, not every week," he said. "If it were anybody but the Baron, his attendance record would be regarded as disgraceful. Actually, he proposed me for membership: I don't think the other members would have dreamed of admitting a policeman if he hadn't sponsored me. We all call him the Baron, whatever my wife says."

"Interesting, how the genes run in those families," said the old man, nodding his head in agreement with himself. "If ever a man had the look of a feudal lord, it was Maeda. Still does, I imagine. Surely he must have retired, though?"

Otani shrugged. "Well, yes and no. He's no longer the President of the Maeda Trading Company, but he's still Chairman of the Board and quite active. Then there's his other interest. He gives a good deal of time to the *bunraku* puppet theatre organisation in Osaka."

Hanae opened her mouth to enlarge on Maeda's enthusiasm for *bunraku* and his generosity in the matter of complimentary tickets but was forestalled by a sudden chuckle from Professor Horiguchi.

"I was wondering where I had got to," he said. "Yes. Boom! Earthquake Johnny's notes. Well, it seems that he gave some thought to ways of predicting earthquakes. Even then they could cause a great deal of damage, though he could scarcely have foreseen the extent of the great Tokyo disaster of my younger days. He used to ride round on a horse talking

9

to farmers and fishermen. And his notes are full of tales about rats running out of storehouses, pigs bolting from their pens and birds behaving oddly for hours and even days before a major seismic event.''

Professor Horiguchi looked from one to the other of his guests in triumph. ''You thought I'd forgotten about the catfish. But I hadn't. I keep up with the literature, you know, I keep up with the literature. And there's no doubt that of all the creatures one may conveniently keep and observe in a laboratory, catfish are quite the cleverest at predicting earthquakes. How strange that the ancient legend has it that earthquakes are *caused* by the restlessness of a gigantic catfish deep in the earth! Anyway, their behaviour patterns are rather striking, and certain types have always and only been noted within quite specific time-limits immediately before a major tremor. I cannot answer your question except with a guess. Water of course is a very sensitive conductor of vibrations. Better than any seismograph. And if an earthquake has its epicentre in the sea-bed, there may well follow a *tsunami* tidal wave. That *would* bother a catfish, my friend!''

The old man sat back. All at once he looked very weary, and Hanae made a sign to Otani that they should make their excuses. Professor Horiguchi intercepted it. ''I fear that I have rambled on,'' he said remorsefully. ''I have gossiped away and not asked you any of your news. No, please don't go just yet. I have few visitors these days, though my former students are extremely thoughtful. You have a young daughter, I believe. How is she? She must be quite a big girl now.''

Hanae smiled. ''Our daughter Akiko is twenty-six and married, sensei,'' she said. ''She has recently become a mother, and we now have a grandson.''

Professor Horiguchi sat bolt upright. ''You, a grandmother? Quite impossible,'' he protested gallantly, and Otani smiled as he stood up.

''My wife is very susceptible to flattery. Horiguchi-sensei,'' he said. ''But I think I must take her away before she succumbs to you. We shall be staying at Ama-no-hashidate for the next two nights. Could we persuade you to come and dine with us at our inn tomorrow?''

The old man's vigour waxed and waned like a light becoming brighter and dimmer with fluctuations in the power supply. Now he looked frail, as he shook his head slowly. "You are more than kind," he said, then paused. "I seldom go out nowadays, and I am generally abed very early. And, you know, I find it rather difficult to sit on the floor these days. So you will perhaps forgive a decrepit old scientist if I stay at home with my books and papers."

He insisted on leading the way to the front door, and stood there for a moment before opening it. "You must come again," he said. "I have so much enjoyed our conversation. Imagine Maeda turning to *bunraku* at his age. Do give him my best wishes. And the earthquakes. I hope you never have one in Kobe, with all those tall office buildings. My word, how Earthquake Johnny would have enjoyed the prospect, though!" The handshakes were firm and the mane of hair was soft and springy as he bade them farewell. Hanae, again disconcerted by the un-Japanese handshake, turned and bowed hesitantly when they reached the outer gate. Professor Horiguchi inclined his head in response, then followed the gesture up with a little wave of the hand.

"We'll find a taxi near the shops, I expect," said Otani. "He doesn't look his age, does he? Even though he did get muddled about the Baron. *Bunraku* puppets are one thing he doesn't manipulate."

Hanae looked at him sidelong. "What a funny thing to say," she murmured. "Whatever do you mean?"

Otani shook his head. "Nothing," he said. "Just a casual remark. For an old man he keeps his fingers in a good many pies." Hanae knew from experience that she would get no more from him on that tack, and hastened her step.

"I thought the old Professor was wonderful," she said. "Look, there's a taxi. Let's hurry and we'll probably have the bath to ourselves."

"So we will," Otani agreed, reflecting that the bath at the Kissei-Ro was a good big one with room for manoeuvre. It was good to be on holiday, with other people back at headquarters doing some work for a change.

Chapter 2

WHILE OTANI AND HANAE WERE WATCHING THE MAID lay out the bedding in their room at the inn, Inspector Noguchi, head of the Hyogo Prefectural Police Drugs Section, was making his way apparently unhurriedly to a divisional police station in the south-east of Kobe. He was in one of the seedier parts of the city but the narrow street he was walking down was bright with gimcrack gaiety. On either side were the red, white and black-lettered paper lantern shades of dozens of tiny food bars, most with their sliding doors open to the warm evening air. A good many offered various kinds of meat dishes broiled over small gas or charcoal ranges, including several advertising "stamina" or "hormone" food in the Korean style.

Noguchi himself enjoyed a good big platter of these tasty bits of garlicky liver, kidney and less mentionable left-overs. from the cattle and pigs which provided the elegant steaks and cutlets served at the classy hotels and restaurants near Sannomiya Station; though he was past caring whether food of that kind really had the aphrodisiac effects claimed for it. The appetising smells drifting from the doors and the convivial sounds he heard made him wish he had an hour or so of time on his hands.

Inspector Noguchi actually had a proper first name. It was one often given to boys coming late into big families, and had a winsome ring to it. All the same it would be a bold and intimate friend who would venture now to address him as Hachiro, or Number Eight. He was some years older than his superior officer Otani, and looked a disgrace. A pair of capacious and grimy trousers, the lower half of what had once been a suit, were secured to his majestic belly by an enormous leather belt, while his barrel chest was encased in a flannel shirt buttoned to the neck but minus a tie. The sleeves were rolled up, and on one beefy forearm a tattooed dragon displayed itself, while a snake decorated the other. In his present surroundings he looked tough but in no other way unusual, and none of the people in the street gave him a second look, except the cook-proprietor of a *yakitori* grilled chicken bar who was putting a crate of empty beer bottles outside as Noguchi passed and who hastily ducked back in as he encountered his bland gaze.

Noguchi paid no particular attention to him, and continued to the end of the street, past a shabby little Turkish bath-house with a pasty-faced girl in shorts and bra lounging in the doorway, and a rather more pretentious coffee-shop with two or three electronic Space Invader games incorporated into the glass-topped tables. Noguchi was mildly surprised to see evidence of the Space Invader craze in this part of town. At a hundred yen a game with no prospect of prizes it had for a year or so constituted a serious problem in the more middle-class areas. College and high-school youngsters seemed to become quickly addicted, and the few who consistently achieved high scores in shooting down the alien spacecraft acquired groups of admiring fans, mostly girls. With expenditure of thousands of yen a session it was a habit difficult to support, though, and a good many were drifting into petty theft, prostitution and even drug-pushing to raise the money for it.

Noguchi was completely in his element in the Kobe half-world and underworld. Having specialised for years in knowing most of what there was to know about it, he could and often did go to ground for days on end in the slums inhabited by the Koreans and the *buraku* or outcast Japanese, and could vanish in seconds in the alleys and sleazy bars of the waterfront. He took a great deal more pride than he would ever admit in the nickname "Ninja" which had been bestowed on him originally by an outraged gangster when Noguchi appeared seemingly from nowhere at the crucial moment of a big pay-off in a quiet suburban house in Akashi years before.

He liked the idea of being thought to have an affinity with the undercover agents of contending *daimyo* in feudal times, believed by common people to possess the power of invisibility at will, and made no objection when the tag began to catch on after his victim referred to him as a confounded *ninja* at the investigation by the District Prosecutor. It was only his closest colleagues who dared to use it to his face, but Noguchi knew that everyone else did so behind his back.

The Duty Inspector at Divisional Headquarters had dealt with Noguchi before, and knew what to expect when he shambled in through the main entrance of the small and crowded two-storey building in the main road which constituted one boundary of the cheap entertainment area from which he had emerged. The police office was alive with people, most of them in uniform, though some of those working at tiny desks in the main open-plan area were wearing slippers, their shoes neatly lined up at the foot of an old fashioned umbrella stand.

At the main enquiry counter an elderly senior patrolman was listening patiently to an incoherent harangue from a skinny, distracted woman who might have been anything from thirty to fifty, while the man with her sat sullenly in a corner, smoking a cigarette and glancing about with occasional flashes of belligerence on his face. The Inspector spotted Noguchi through the open door of the small office he occupied near the counter, and came out to usher him inside. He was a tall, scholarly-looking man with glasses, whose uniform seemed out of place as the two of them sat down in the little room, the door still open.

Noguchi glanced at the woman. She was wearing a limp cotton Western-style dress and cheap high-heeled shoes with one strap broken and flapping round her unappetising ankle. She had not stopped talking but had now produced a dirty bit of rag with which she was dabbing at her reddened eyes. "What's all that about?" he said. The Inspector followed his glance and smiled briefly. "Oh nothing," he said casually. "Those two come in once or twice a week. She wants him to marry her, that's all. They only come when that particular patrolman's on duty. He's a wonder with them. Listens quietly, calms her down, and away they go after a while. Then in a day or two he'll complain she isn't bringing in enough money, knock her about a bit and they'll be back." The Inspector shrugged, and took off his glasses and polished them carefully with a paper handkerchief before replacing them and continuing. "We get plenty like that. What I've got for you is new to me, though. I'm glad you could come."

Noguchi nodded, then scratched his nose. "Where have you put him? In the tiger-box?" he asked.

The Inspector shook his head. "No room. We've got a howling drunk in there already. No, we've put this lad in the ordinary pig-box cell. It has a bunk and chair in it, mainly because we don't have to hose it down practically every night." He reached over to the small filing-cabinet at his side, unlocked it and took out a gun, which he laid on the low table in front of Noguchi.

Noguchi looked at it without picking it up. "So?" he grunted. "Seen one before, I take it?"

The Inspector declined to be put down by his visitor. "I don't pick up too many Gun Control Law cases," he said calmly, "but I wouldn't come running to you if that was the whole of it. Wait till you see the kid before implying I'm wasting your time. And have a closer look at the shooter."

With another sceptical grunt Noguchi reached out and picked up the revolver with one hand, then transferred it to the other while he first peered at his palm then wiped it on his trouser leg. Dirty as his trousers were, his action left a greasy mark. Then Noguchi looked more closely at the gun, and broke into what was for him eloquent speech. "This is brand new," he said incredulously. "Original greasing. And loaded. Did the damn young fool want to blow his hand apart?''

The Inspector looked at Noguchi with some satisfaction. ''It's quite obvious to me that he's never handled one before in his life. And what I think we ought to find out is where he got hold of it. As well as why he wanted it.''

Noguchi nodded. ''What sort of a boy is he?''

''Come and see for yourself.''

He stood up. Noguchi followed suit, and the Inspector led the way through the main office towards the back of the building. As he predicted, the woman at the counter had fallen silent but was still scrubbing at her eyes and sniffing as the patrolman spoke quietly to her and her pimp fidgeted on his chair. The identity of the Inspector's visitor must have been whispered among those who had never seen him before, and a few heads turned for a discreet look at the famous Ninja Noguchi as he shuffled through the room.

The occupant of the bare ''tiger-box'' provided for violent drunks was setting up a considerable racket, his sporadic shouts and curses interspersed with occasional snatches of song and cackles of laughter. Noguchi peered in through the barred window as they passed. Inured as he was to the seamier aspects of police work, it came as something of a surprise to him to see not an unshaven day-labourer with a quart of the cheapest *shochu* potato spirit in him, but a middle-class salaryman complete with document case. Though in disorder, his clothes were respectable and of good quality, and the flushed distorted face was one of character. He'd have some explaining to do at home and the office at the end of what looked like a two-day drunk.

The ''pig-box'' next door was quiet; and when the two men entered, the boy sitting on the edge of the bunk raised his head but said nothing. His dress and general appearance would have gone unremarked in any of the places where young people who follow the latest in pop fashions congregate. He looked to Noguchi to be about eighteen or nineteen, and was wearing tight bright yellow cotton jeans, socks with green and yellow diagonal stripes, and clean white canvas shoes. Covering his scrawny chest was a T-shirt in plain green with some

16

English words printed on it and the stripes of an American army sergeant on one arm. His coarse hair was cut short and stood up in irregular spikes on his head, and in front had been either dyed or sprayed yellow. He had severe acne all over his face and neck, and his mouth and chin were weak.

"Scares the pants off you, doesn't he?" said Noguchi not unkindly to the Inspector and the boy scowled and looked down again.

The Inspector gestured to the plain wooden chair, then sat in it himself when Noguchi waved it away and remained upright near the door. The Inspector cleared his throat as he produced a folded sheet of paper from the pocket of his tunic, then began to speak. "Right. I'm going to read through the statement you made earlier. We haven't asked you to sign it yet, and this officer may have some more questions to ask. You'll be asked to sign after we've finished, but you know we can't oblige you to do so. You're still a minor, but you're over eighteen, and the charge is in respect of an offence carrying a sentence of over three years. You can get up to seven for violating the Weapons Possession Law.

"So we don't need a warrant. You can be held here for up to forty-eight hours while we decide whether we need to refer your case to the prosecutor. It's up to you. If you have any second thoughts while I read your statement, we can tear it up and take another. Understand?"

The boy nodded in silence. "Right. 'My name is Oda, Hiroshi, of 20–16 Higashi-machi, Kami-ku, Takeda City, Hyogo Prefecture. I was nineteen years old on 17 February last, and I live with my parents. I left high school in April last year but failed the entrance examinations for university. I attend a private *juku* preparatory school and intend to take the entrance examinations again. On Thursday 26 April I was with some friends at the New International Disco and Pub in Kobe City. I arrived at about 7 pm. At about 8 pm I became angry with one of my friends who insulted me. I wanted to frighten him and took out a toy pistol which I had in my shoulder bag. A man came over and said he was a police officer. He took the toy gun and arrested me and brought me here. He said it was a real gun but I know it is not. I have

17

done nothing wrong. I have nothing more to say.' That is the end of the statement.''

The Inspector raised his eyes from the paper and looked at Noguchi, who had remained completely immobile throughout. Noguchi spoke.

"You can get three years for intimidation, son," he said quietly. "Even if it had been a toy. Are you suggesting the officer who brought you here substituted another gun for yours?" The head was still lowered, but there was the slightest movement of negation. "Maybe you honestly *thought* it was a toy," Noguchi rumbled on. "Maybe we'll believe you. Maybe not. Where did you get it, and why were you carrying it?" The boy said nothing, but shook his head again.

The Inspector took up the questioning, after looking at his watch. "It's still quite early," he said. "Only just after ten-thirty. Still, we shall have to make contact with your parents before long. Why not help us? You'll only make it worse by refusing. If you really thought it was a toy and could prove that, it would help you. First of all, though, where did you get it?"

Oda looked up, weaselly in his confusion and fright. "I found it," he said at last in a thin unattractive voice that went with his appearance.

Noguchi belched briefly, making no more than the most perfunctory sketch of covering his mouth. "Where?" he demanded.

"I can't remember," muttered the boy after a hesitation. The two policemen looked at each other, the one with an expression of alert academic interest, the other in gloomy impatience.

"You found it," said Noguchi then in a voice of heavy irony. "You found it. In a plastic basket in the supermarket? Under your chair in the classroom? Among your mother's knickers? Come on, lad, don't waste our time. You're in trouble. Want to make it big trouble? "

The boy coloured. "I thought it was a toy," he said doggedly. "I found it in a drawer. In a man's house, with some bullets. I thought it was one of those copies you used to be able to buy before they made them illegal." He sniffed,

18

and looked even younger and more incongruous in his tawdry finery than he had before. "I didn't mean any harm," he almost wailed.

"You just wanted to impress your friends," suggested the Inspector helpfully. Oda looked at him as though he might be a potential ally, and nodded.

"Coming on," said Noguchi grimly. "So you stole it. Larceny. That's even worse. Up to ten years." He heaved a massive sigh, and turned his bleak gaze to his colleague. "If this lad wants to keep away from the Prosecutor, Inspector," he said in formal tones, "it seems to me he'd better tell the truth. And a bit more besides."

The Inspector nodded. "That's so," he said to the boy. "At this stage we have a certain amount of discretion. If you can satisfy us that you honestly thought the gun was a dummy, we *might* decide to believe you. And if you took it for a lark, intending to give it back, that might help you too. We won't begin to credit your story if you don't tell us everything, though. You can start by telling us where you found the gun, and when. A man's house, you said. Where? What man? His name, and the address."

Hiroshi Oda, aged nineteen, looked from the mild-mannered Inspector in his uniform of authority to the menacing figure of Ninja Noguchi at the door, and began to crumple almost visibly. "I don't *know*," he began, on the verge of tears. "All I know is that he was a foreigner. . . ."

Chapter 3

Bᴏʏs' Dᴀʏ ꜰᴇʟʟ ᴏɴ ᴀ Sᴀᴛᴜʀᴅᴀʏ ᴛʜᴀᴛ ʏᴇᴀʀ. Iᴛ ᴅᴀᴡɴᴇᴅ beautifully, and when the sun came up over the Wakayama peninsula, darting its shafts across the Inland Sea and among the shaggy wooded folds and crevices of Mount Rokko, it was justification enough for the day's pride of place at the end of Golden Week.

The Otanis lived in one of the oldest suburban areas between Kobe and Osaka, in the last of a cluster of wooden houses quite high among the Rokko foothills. Otani stood at the open window of the upstairs room in which they slept, and which doubled as the formal reception room for company. The Inland Sea was in clear view a mile or so away, and even at that early hour the first white passenger ferry was moving on the glassy surface of the water. Probably full of day trippers on their way to Awaji Island, Otani thought, transferring his gaze from the boat, tiny in the distance, to the huddled grey and blue tiled rooftops of the houses below, the commuter railway lines, and the Osaka–Kobe highway between his vantage point and the sea.

There was obviously no shortage of boys in their district. Over a surprisingly high proportion of the rooftops fluttered the proud carp streamers, like the windsocks still seen at small airfields, their bright blues and reds cheerful in the early morning sunshine. With so many factories closed for the entire holiday week the air was much cleaner than usual, and Otani sniffed at the freshness with pleasure.

Hanae finished folding up their bedding and stowing it in the big cupboard beside the *tokonoma*, and came and joined him at the window for a moment.

"The carp streamers look nice," Otani said. "I rather wish we had put some up for little Kazuo-chan after all."

Hanae smiled. "It would have been cheating," she said. "You know quite well that it's only if you have a little boy actually in the house that you're supposed to fly them. And you did buy the most enormous ones in the shop for Akira to put up."

Otani nodded. "It still doesn't seem quite the same when you see about ten sets all side by side on top of a block of flats though."

"Come and have breakfast," said Hanae, moving towards the stairs. "If you're really going to the office on a holiday again and a Saturday too you can at least begin with *hammu eggu*. And don't worry about your grandson. He'll be able to swim upstream as strongly as any carp."

Otani lingered over the panoramic view he never tired of before following Hanae to the kitchen, where she had already started to fry a slice of bright pink processed ham and was breaking an egg over it.

The first tremor came as Otani was spreading marmalade on his second piece of toast. It was of sufficient strength to slop some of the coffee in his full cup into the saucer, and was accompanied by a heavy, lurching rumble as though a huge overloaded juggernaut lorry were impossibly speeding along past their house. "*Ara!* That was a big one," he said in some surprise, and looked up at Hanae, who was standing as though transfixed. "Not frightened, are you?" he said. Earth tremors were so familiar a feature of life that only the severer ones, like this, even occasioned comment. Their house creaked and swayed once or twice most weeks, and always seemed to adjust itself comfortably again to the restless earth.

Hanae carefully put down the kettle she had been holding. "No, not frightened," she said. "It's just that I nearly spilled boiling water on my foot." She found a cloth and mopped up the puddle from the floor. "Strange that we should have been talking about earthquakes just last week," she said. "I wonder if the catfish knew this one was coming."

"Hardly," said Otani, reassured that no harm had come to Hanae. "That wasn't really an earthquake, just an everyday tremor. If the poor creatures react every time to that sort of thing they must lead very neurotic lives."

They settled back into their morning routine, the shock soon forgotten in the general sense of unreality caused by the extended Sunday quiet of the public holidays. "I told Tomita to come for me half an hour later than usual," said Otani when he noticed Hanae glance at the clock in a meaning way. "Traffic will be light, and in any case I can't believe there'll be much in the way of paperwork for me today."

"Poor Tomita-san," said Hanae. "It seems a shame to make him work through Golden Week too."

Otani smiled briefly. "No need for sympathy. You know how he hates to let anybody else drive my car. His car, actually, I suppose. Especially that lunatic Sato. No, Tomita was quite happy to take his holiday when we did. On the whole it's been rather a pleasant week for us martyrs on duty."

Otani made the same point to his official driver as he piloted the black and white Toyota Police Special down the narrow winding lanes towards the main road, and Patrolman Tomita agreed wholeheartedly. Both men were in civilian clothes, Tomita by Otani's special dispensation which as usual he had interpreted liberally. In honour of the public holiday he was sporting a shiny bright blue zippered jerkin over an open-necked shirt, sporty-looking trousers, and brown and white footwear of the kind once known as co-respondent shoes.

Otani was wearing his usual unobtrusive dark suit, a white shirt, and one of the few ties in his collection which looked even slightly different from all the others. This one was rather dashing, with club stripes, and had been given to him by one of the English delegates to an Interpol conference held in Kyoto some years before. Otani had not quite understood the interpreter's explanation, and believed the design to represent the insignia of Scotland Yard. He was very proud of the tie, but he was in error: it was in fact that of the Metropolitan Police Operatic Society.

"You'd better not let Inspector Kimura see you in those clothes," said Otani affably. "He might think you're trying to out-do him." Tomita smiled broadly, revealing two gold teeth, and deprecatingly denied any ambition to emulate the Inspector, who was usually referred to by the patrolmen among themselves as Pretty Boy. They continued to chat in a desultory way during the remainder of the drive, which was indeed markedly shorter and less difficult than on a normal working day. There were plenty of private cars on the roads, many of them obviously containing whole families off for the day to popular picnic spots; others bearing men only, with golf bags or fishing gear much in evidence. It was the absence of heavy goods vehicles that really made the difference, and Otani found himself whistling tunelessly as he made his way into the headquarters building of the Hyogo Prefectural Police Force near the harbour in the oldest part of Kobe.

He acknowledged the stiff salute of the uniformed man on duty at the door and made his way up the broad staircase to the second-floor corridor with its central strip of fraying coconut matting and framed photographs of his predecessors, and to the lofty double doors with the identification board sticking out like a little signpost at right angles to the wall.

OTANI Tetsuo
Commanding Officer

The white painted Chinese characters on the black panel never caught his eye nowadays, though they had drawn his gaze like a magnet in the first few months after the Governor had formally appointed him on behalf of the Public Safety Commission. In one sense the summit of an ambition; in another the beginning of the final stage of a career.

Otani walked into the big, ugly room, the air dull and frowsty in keeping with the general atmosphere of inactivity in the building, and looked around him with a sudden sense of dissatisfaction. It really was a very dreary office, in a gloomy pile of a headquarters, though it must have been thought very grand at one time. Built of brick in the brief reign of the poor degenerate Taisho Emperor sixty years earlier, the edifice over which he presided was certainly impressive in scale. Otani continued to brood quietly as he opened a window with a view over part of the harbour, put his jacket tidily on a wire hanger and suspended it from the coatstand in the corner, sat at the ornate desk and shuffled through the pile of papers on the plain sheet of glass which he preferred as a writing surface.

Of course, in those days Osaka was unquestionably the principal mercantile centre in the area and had been for centuries, but it had not yet wrested from Kobe the status of chief modern city of Western Japan, the historical centre of international trade in that part of the country and, in the days before commercial air transport, the only serious competitor to Yokohama and Nagasaki among the main ports.

Now the mighty but somehow eternally upstart city of Osaka with its brash, money-making reputation and skyscraper office buildings was the only real alternative centre of gravity to Tokyo. Even though there was no longer any countryside in the twenty miles that separated the two cities, Otani could always feel the difference when he left Osaka's drab featureless sprawl and came back into his own patch.

Maybe Kobe *had* decayed, relatively. Maybe he *was* left only with the Americans and the honorary consuls of banana republics doubling as managers of foreign banks and shipping agencies while the other big boys, the British, Russians, Germans and others, had set up steel and glass and chromium-plated Consulate Generals in Osaka. Kobe was still a real place, though, with proper temples and shrines, not to mention an ornate Islamic mosque; some fine old houses among the blocks of expensive flats in the part near the Kobe Club where the important foreigners used to live, good shops and restaurants and a prosperous if unaggressive commercial community.

No. On reflection, Otani did not envy his opposite number in Osaka Prefecture next door, for all his fancy new building, computer centre, helicopter pad and the rest of it. On an impulse he pressed the buzzer on his telephone. Normally his clerk appeared within seconds of the summons; but today answer came there none. Otani waited, momentarily puzzled, and was about to buzz again when he remembered the holiday and shook his head in despair at his own forgetfulness. He picked up the receiver and dialed the switchboard.

No delays there. The operator had a special indicator on Otani's extension, and he responded almost instantaneously. "Who is supposed to be looking after me today?" Otani demanded a little crossly.

"I'll connect you with the duty room, sir," the operator barked, anxious to get the Old Man off his hands immediately. There followed a series of clicking noises, then the familiar tones of Ninja Noguchi, who could never quite bring himself to address Otani formally, though furiously castigating anybody else who referred to him in his hearing with less than the most scrupulous propriety.

Otani was pleased to hear him, and his brief irritation dissolved as the voice said, "Morning. You're bright and early."

"Ninja," he said. "I'd forgotten you were back today. Good morning to you. Busy?"

"Not really. One or two things. Shall I come up?"

"Do. And see if you can find somebody in this mausoleum to sit in my outer office for the day, will you? I seem to have had somebody different every day this week, but the system's broken down today. And whoever it is can bring some tea, perhaps."

He put the telephone down and looked through the day's haul of incoming papers as he waited. Very dull stuff. Circulars from the Ministry of Justice, notification of the appointment of new assistant judges to the District Court, an invitation to a road safety exhibition organised by the Ibaraki

Housewives' League . . . but then he scarcely expected anything else. Might just as well have stayed at home.

The door opened and Inspector Noguchi entered, propelling a frightened-looking junior constable before him. The young man bore a tin tray on which were a small kettle and two handleless cups. He kept trying to stop in order to come to attention, and Noguchi remorselessly frustrated every attempt. "Put it down there, son," he growled, indicating a low table set with geometrical precision in a group of easy chairs, "then make yourself scarce in the ante-room next door." The policeman did as he was bidden, and made for the door.

"Just a moment. Thank you, Constable," said Otani politely. "What is your name? I don't think I've seen you about, have I?"

At last the boy was able to stand to attention, and did so gratefully. "Migishima, sir," he said. "I have just completed basic training."

Otani nodded. "Good. I hope you will work hard and successfully here. Now do the best you can next door, and if you don't understand anything, ask." As Migishima went out of the communicating door Noguchi bellowed after him to jump to it if he heard the Chief's buzzer go; then the door closed and silence fell as the two old colleagues looked at each other.

Noguchi's bullet head moved slightly in a minimal bow, and Otani returned the nod before either of them spoke. "Seems a likely sort of lad," said Noguchi then, jerking a thumb towards the door.

"I'm sure that you're making him feel thoroughly at home, Ninja," Otani said, amiably sarcastic. "With your inimitable charm. Good morning to you. It's good to see you again." He stood up, crossed to the table and poured out two cups of green tea, handing one to Noguchi. "Not your drink, I know, but it's still pretty early," he said.

Noguchi took his cup in silence, and as he sipped the aromatic tea he drank by the pint every day, Otani looked him up and down. Presumably at some stage in his career as a police officer Ninja must have possessed a uniform, and by all the laws of probability would have been obliged to wear it at least occasionally. In the ten years Otani had known him, however, he had seen him on four or five occasions in a decent suit, but never dressed up as a policeman. The very idea was ridiculous. Most often he looked as he did now, like a beery ex-sumo wrestler gone thoroughly to seed.

Noguchi's face was an impenetrable mask of crags and crevices. It was really not at all surprising that his efforts to shave were seldom crowned with much success and that he usually displayed two to three days' growth of stubble. The real mystery was that it tended to remain at that stage, and Otani occasionally wondered idly how the effect was achieved. In two or three years at most Ninja would have to retire. For Otani, it would be like losing a limb.

"Well, Ninja," he enquired at last, "what's new? Or did you tidy everything up neatly before you went off?"

Noguchi hadn't much in the way of neck, and what little there was disappeared as he shrugged massively. "Only one thing worth mentioning," he said. "Otherwise small stuff on my side. Pickpockets. That kind of thing, when you're expecting something more interesting. Enjoy yourselves, did you?"

"Very much, thank you. So another quiet day to finish off the week, perhaps?"

Noguchi put his cup down. He had hardly touched his tea. "I should think so," he agreed. "Traffic boys will be busy. Usual pile-ups, Sunday drivers, drunks."

There was a pause, then Otani put his own cup down and sank into one of the easy chairs. "All right, Ninja," he said. "Let's have it. 'Only one thing worth mentioning,' you said."

Noguchi lowered himself into another chair, poked a finger through a gap left by a missing shirt button and scratched himself in the region of his navel. "Wish Kimura was here," he confessed surprisingly. He normally professed such dismissive scorn for Kimura and all his works that for a moment Otani thought he had imagined the remark. It was also rare for Noguchi to embark on anything in the nature of an extended narrative, and Otani remained silent as he gave an account of his visit the previous week to the Divisional

Headquarters at the request of the Duty Inspector, the interview with Hiroshi Oda and the peculiar condition of the gun, which had been sent for examination to the regional forensic laboratory.

Needless to say, it became clear as Noguchi went on that he had taken no holiday at all but had been prodding about quietly on the case, and that even Kimura had been interested enough to work on it with him right up to the last minute before flying off to Taiwan. The laboratory tests revealed only Oda's prints on the bullets, and the fact that the gun had been incorrectly loaded and was indeed in a highly dangerous condition. What was more to the point was that the serial number indicated that it was of quite recent European manufacture.

After a while Noguchi stopped, and Otani put some of the questions that had occurred to him while listening to the story. "Has this gone any further yet?" he asked first. It looked as though the National Police Agency investigators might have to be brought in at some stage.

Noguchi shook his head. "No. I've kept it to myself, and told the lab people to keep quiet about it. Brought Kimura in on the business of the foreigner. We've let the boy go home on bail to his family for the time being. Miserable little snot, but no real harm in him. No great loss if he had blown himself to bits, but on the whole we believe him. Kimura talked to him for a long time about the foreigner. Apparently picked young Oda and three or four other youngsters up late one night and took them to a house somewhere between here and Osaka. They were pretty far gone and he probably really doesn't remember exactly where it was. Offered them a fair bit of money to let him take photos of them all on the job—there were a couple of girls there. They sobered up at this and tried to get out of it, but he raised the ante and eventually they went along with it. Plenty of drink in the process, and two or three dozen pictures taken they wouldn't want to show their mothers. Our lad goes to be sick in the bathroom, and has a bit of a look round when he feels better. Finds what he says he thought was a fake gun and some dummy bullets and thinks he can cut a bit of a dash with it. Stows it away."

"How did the youngsters leave the house? Middle of the

28

night? Not too easy.'' Otani wasted no emotion on the sordid little story and had a detached, interested expression on his face.

''The foreigner paid them off, drove them back into town, dropped them at Sannomiya with their fifty thousand yen apiece in their grubby little hands and left them to it. About two in the morning by then, it seems.''

''What about the other boys, and the girls? Have they been identified? Description of the foreigner from any of them?''

Noguchi shook his head. ''Kimura tried to follow that up. Oda said he didn't know their names. Crowds of kids go to dance at that disco; pick each other up and drop each other just like that. Local plainclothes lads are sniffing about trying to find anyone who admits to knowing Oda, but nothing so far. We're dependent on Oda's description. All he claims to remember is that he was a European who spoke good Japanese. Old, he said, and heavily built. Nasty bit of work by the sound of it. Tried to get them to beat one of the girls just for fun.'' Noguchi sighed. ''Well, we haven't got very far. Kimura's been through his files of foreign residents in the whole area between Kobe and Osaka. There are hundreds of them, and dozens of middle-aged or older men. None of them has any record involving porno pictures, still less gun-dealing.''

''Still,'' said Otani reasonably, ''there can't be too many middle-aged European men who speak good Japanese in the area. Kimura-kun may be able to reduce the list to a few, and we could start keeping an eye on possibles. The man will surely have been worried by the loss of the gun. Do you really think that he may be a dealer, then?''

The question was hanging between them when there was a hesitant tapping at the door, and both men looked round in surprise as it opened slowly and the youthful features of Constable Migishima came into view. Noguchi prepared to roar at him, then relapsed into his chair as Otani caught his eye. ''What is it, Constable?'' said Otani mildly. The young man's embarrassment was painful to see.

''There is no excuse for my intrusion, sir,'' he blurted out, ''but I couldn't make the telephone work and there was nobody about to ask. There is a call for the Superintendent, from a Mr Horiguchi in Miyazu. He is most anxious to speak to you, sir. He has already tried the Superintendent's house.'' He veered uncertainly between the second and third persons in his anxiety to convey both urgency and regard for protocol in his language.

"All right, I'll take it in the outer office," said Otani. "Afterwards I'll show you how to switch the extension through. Don't go away, Ninja." He went out of the room, leaving Noguchi glowering at an apprehensive Migishima.

He was gone for some time, during which interval Noguchi gave the fledgling policeman a caustic grounding in some of the fundamentals of his trade which Migishima was never to forget. When Otani did come back into the room, Migishima's principal emotion was one of relief as he prepared to make his escape; but it was not to be. Otani looked perfectly relaxed and calm, but there was a contained tension about him which imposed itself on the whole atmosphere of the room.

"You'd better stay—Migishima, isn't it?—you may be in for a busy day, young man," said Otani quietly. "Sit down and get your notebook out." The dead, empty holiday quiet of the normally bustling building and the absence of the usual heavy traffic in the port approach roads somehow emphasised the reflective, even tones in which Otani first explained who Professor Horiguchi was and then gave the other two men a brief account of his conversation with the old scientist the previous week.

"I tell you this merely to forestall any questions, and to explain why it is that we have some time to prepare ourselves before the Meteorological Agency alerts the Prefectural Government—if they can find anybody there—and we have to go into action. Dr Horiguchi felt this morning's tremor up there on the Japan Sea, and the same thought crossed his mind as occurred to my wife—he wondered if the catfish had behaved in any way oddly." Otani paused to pour himself another cup of the now tepid green tea, and the other two watched him in silence.

"He has a former pupil who runs the seismological research station at Suma, a few kilometres west of us, and he decided to give him a ring, expecting to find him at home. He wasn't there, and Horiguchi-sensei eventually tracked him down at the lab. He found out two things. First, the epicentre of this morning's shock was in the Inland Sea near Awaji, and that it was about Three on the Richter Scale; not enough to cause a significant tidal wave. And no, the behaviour of the catfish over the last two or three days was nothing out of the ordinary. They don't react *after* a shock, so you'd expect them to be quite normal. But they aren't. They are at this moment demonstrating patterns of stress activity which suggest that a major earthquake will take place within the next twenty-four hours with an epicentre somewhere in Western Japan.''

Noguchi sat in rock-like impassivity, almost as though challenging a mere earthquake to shift him. ''Bit out of my line,'' he observed. ''Anything I can do?''

Migishima looked from one to the other of his two superiors. His mind still confused from the tongue-lashing he had received from the terrifying old bruiser who seemed to be on such good terms with the Chief, he had, when first Otani began to speak, wondered if he had strayed into some surrealist comedy, a victim of an elaborate joke devised for some unfathomable reason by the pair of them. Now he changed mental gear, and began to think of the practical implications of the prediction Otani had passed on.

''A good deal depends on how seriously the Governor's office takes any warning from the Meteorological Agency,'' said Otani. ''There's some talk about a new committee of experts with access to the Prime Minister since the change in the law last December, but it hasn't started functioning yet. There are still a lot of officials about who are very skeptical about predictions, and when you consider it's one of the big holidays of the year . . .'' He shrugged. ''I'll talk to the Governor's office and try to get an idea of the line they'll take. If someone with enough seniority is willing to stick his neck out, they'll declare a full-scale alert and we'll have an official liaison rôle between the Ground Self-Defence Forces, fire services, hospitals and so on. That will mean bringing as many of our own men as possible back from leave, warning

31

our own Divisional Headquarters up and down the Prefecture, and so on and so forth. Ninja, you'd better get the men in the duty room to contact Fire Headquarters and the main hospitals to let them know there may be an official alert.''

Noguchi hauled himself out of his chair and hitched up his voluminous trousers. ''And suppose the Governor's office pooh-pooh it?'' he said, looking down at Otani. Migishima had scrambled hastily to his feet as Noguchi rose.

Otani still looked very composed. ''Then we must do all we can by ourselves,'' he said. ''The biggest danger is fire, and the most vulnerable areas are the slums. That would be very much in your line, Ninja. It'll be up to you to get hold of the *yakuza* bosses and get them to pass the word down the line to their various local link men. They carry more authority in those areas than any police loudspeaker van, and they'll get the word round faster.''

Otani stood up as well. ''Set up a small operations centre in the duty room, Ninja,'' he said. ''I'll join you down there in half an hour. Migishima and I have one or two calls to make from here first.'' Otani watched Noguchi as he left the room, then turned and scrutinised Migishima thoroughly for the first time. He was a tough-looking young man in spite of his obvious nervousness, and Otani was pleased to note that he wore the uniform rather than the uniform wearing him, as was so often the case with new recruits.

''Don't be misled either by Inspector Noguchi's manner or by his appearance, Migishima,'' he said. ''If you ever develop a quarter of his professionalism you may be well pleased with yourself. He takes my word for it about this warning I've had. Do you?''

''I believe it, sir,'' Migishima said, looking him reasonably straight in the eye.

''Where do your family live, Constable?'' Otani said, returning the boy's gaze.

''In Nada ward, sir.''

''Right. Come with me.''

He led Migishima into the ante-room and showed him how to switch his own extension through from the master instrument. ''I'm going to ring my wife now,'' he said. ''I suggest that you use this other telephone and speak to your family if they're at home. Tell them to disconnect all electrical and gas appliances, stow things away as securely as possible, and take a picnic meal and plenty of drinking water to some open area. *Not* the zoo. And by the way, if you find Inspector Noguchi surprising, wait till you meet Inspector Kimura.'' He nodded, smiled briefly, and went back into his own office to speak to Hanae. It would be a simple matter to make their own house reasonably secure, and in spite of the near miss with the boiling water earlier he was not seriously worried about Hanae. Their daughter Akiko, her husband and the baby presented a different problem. They lived in a fourth-floor flat in a newish block in Kobe itself. Whatever they did about their own flat, if fire broke out below them there could be a disaster.

Hanae took some time to answer, and Otani was about to hang up and wonder what to do next when he finally heard her voice. She explained that she had been gossiping with the neighbours, and had begun to pass on the gist of the conversation when Otani cut in and quickly told her what had happened. Akira and Akiko Shimizu had no telephone, like countless young people in newly developed housing areas. ''I don't feel I can justify sending a police car,'' Otani said eventually. ''Especially when we're so stretched here today. I think you'd better get down there by taxi as soon as you can and take them all back with you to the house. Can you persuade them to go, do you think?''

Hanae was in no doubt. Akiko had as strong a personality as her husband, the former revolutionary student firebrand turned businessman. In Akiko's case, marriage and motherhood had modulated her doctrinaire Maoism into a tough and pragmatic technique for ordering priorities. The Shimizus would certainly revise whatever plans they might have for the weekend in the interests of Master Kazuo Shimizu's well-being. Otani rang off, then told the switchboard operator to connect him with the office of the Governor of Hyogo Prefecture. There was not the slightest prospect of finding His Excellency at work on a Saturday at the end of Golden Week, and Otani had never previously had occasion to test the Prefectural Government's emergency arrangements on a public holiday.

Chapter 4

"IT WAS A REVELATION," HE SAID TO NOGUCHI HALF an hour later in the big ground-floor duty room. Noguchi had mustered half a dozen assorted uniformed and plainclothes men, and had cleared a desk for Otani beside the big wall-map of the Prefecture and neighbouring areas, but Otani drew him aside to one corner of the room to talk to him in relative privacy.

"First I got through to some senile lunatic who seemed to be the resident janitor and thought I was the local patrolman from the corner police box. He kept telling me that it's a holiday today and I eventually persuaded him that I knew that. I asked to speak to the senior duty officer. There isn't one. At least, not officially, but the old chap thought there might be one or two people in the building. After a lot of ringing round, a young woman who sounded like a rational human being answered and seemed to grasp the point that we might have an emergency on our hands. She gave me the number of the Governor's Chief Secretary, and I spoke to him at home. The Governor is leading a fact-finding mission in Hawaii if you please, and the Vice-Governor's in Tokyo on a private holiday. The Chief Secretary leaves it all to us. Has every confidence, you'll be glad to hear, but considers that

35

scientific claims about earthquake predictions are a lot of rubbish. So it's on my head one way or the other.''

Noguchi snorted, and the two men walked back to the centre of the room, where Otani addressed the little company. Migishima hovered at his elbow, notebook in hand and determination in every feature. Otani was concise and straightforward. The unusual nature of the warning called for a very delicate touch. It might be necessary to mobilise all public services to cope with a major disaster; equally it might prove to be a false alarm. All Divisional Headquarters were to be advised—not instructed—to follow suit. Hospital casualty departments in all sizable towns in the Prefecture were to be warned, and the prefectural police duty rooms in neighbouring Osaka, Okayama and Kyoto Prefectures were to be advised of the steps being taken in Hyogo.

. ''That's as much as we can do officially for the present,'' Otani concluded. ''Unofficially, I advise you all to use the first five minutes after I've finished to warn your own families and tell them to pass the word on. Migishima, you will talk to all local radio and television stations. Tell them Hyogo Police always take Meteorological Agency warnings with the utmost seriousness. We consider there is no cause for public alarm but would urge all citizens to take sensible precautions, particularly against fire. And to prepare an emergency food and water supply. The public services are fully prepared for any eventuality at all times.'' Otani raised his eyes heavenwards as he said the last few words, and a ripple of laughter ran round the handful of men listening.

Otani turned to Noguchi. ''Inspector, please put your unofficial information network into top gear. We can't afford to ignore this warning. We were lucky to get it.''

''If the Superintendent will permit . . .'' came the hesitant words from Constable Migishima.

''Yes, what is it?'' Otani's tone was forbidding.

''Sir, we've had only an unofficial warning as yet. The Meteorological Agency haven't been in touch.''

Otani stared at him bleakly, and his voice was smooth and cold. ''You have your instructions, officer. You will carry them out until such time as you receive new ones from Inspector Noguchi or myself. Carry on, Ninja.'' He turned on his heel and walked to the other side of the room. The young idiot could be right. He would lose a great deal of face if nothing came of old Horiguchi's well-intentioned call, and if word got round later—as it would—that Otani had put the entire Prefecture on red alert because an old family friend had taken an interest in the behaviour of some fish. He might have done better to concentrate on Ninja Noguchi's interesting case. He turned and surveyed the scene he had just left. Most of the men in the room were on the telephone, Noguchi on his feet with the body of the instrument tucked under one arm, the receiver imprisoned in his bull neck, leaving both hands free to flip through a battered black notebook as he spoke. Migishima was speaking earnestly on another line. The clock on the wall indicated eleven-seventeen. Well, it was too late to back down now.

At twelve-thirty there had still been no message from the Agency, and Otani sent out for some box lunches for those who had not brought their own. It was with some difficulty that he maintained his habitual composure, and commended Migishima for enterprise in alerting the Kobe Port Superintendent's office and the Coastguard. One of the men had a portable radio with him, and Otani was able to hear for himself that local bulletins incorporated a statement along the lines of his message.

''Needless to say, I shall be delighted if it turns out to have been a false alarm. Nobody in his senses *wants* a disaster,'' Otani was saying to Noguchi through a mouthful of rice and pickles when the National Police Agency came on the line to declare a state of alert. It was three minutes to one, and there followed twenty minutes of feverish activity before an unearthly hush suddenly fell over them all. Years later Otani was still occasionally trying and failing to describe the sensation; something very vaguely like a collective *frisson*, as though a gigantic shadow had fallen over them all, or they were in the audience at a horror film at the most bloodcurdling moment.

Then came a huge, weird sound, a cross between a protracted thunderclap, a mighty organ note and a dreadful groan, as though the very earth were convulsed in death agonies. The solid concrete floor bucked and lurched beneath their feet, the fluorescent lights went out, and Otani was flung violently to the floor. Practically stunned, he was dimly conscious of the continued heaving of the floor as well as of a great weight above him. There was a metallic crash as a filing-cabinet toppled over, the sound of breaking glass and falling plaster, and then the convulsive lurching seemed to stop. "Are you all right, sir?" someone enquired tentatively directly into his ear, and the bulky form of Migishima rolled off him, allowing him to breathe naturally.

As Otani sat up, still slightly dazed, he saw that some at least of the lights had come on again and observed a very rare spectacle: Ninja Noguchi with a broad smile on his face. "Proper little hero we've acquired," he remarked, scratching the back of his red neck. "He was on top of you in no time flat. Only trouble is that most of the rest of us are still on our feet." He extended his ham-like hands and pulled them both up from the floor. "Pretty good, son," he said more kindly to Migishima, who was now suffused with a rich glow of embarrassment.

Otani dusted himself down and looked at Migishima. The young man was indeed smothered in fallen plaster, and might easily have suffered serious injuries in an attempt to protect him if the ceiling had given way. "Thank you, Constable," he said tersely. "Even if you did take me by surprise." He looked round. The room was a mess, but the ceiling seemed to be basically intact, and they had electricity. "There may be another," he said to nobody in particular. "Put yourselves next to the main pillars, and stay there for the next fifteen minutes. If there is another shock and the ceiling begins to go, dive under the nearest desk."

Noguchi made no attempt to move as the others distributed themselves about the room, picking up as they went chairs and some of the books, files and papers that littered the floor.

"How long did it last, Ninja?" Otani asked. "It seemed like minutes on end."

Noguchi wrinkled his nose. "No more than twenty seconds. Seventeen or eighteen perhaps. Don't remember one like it in my lifetime, though. Think there *will* be another?''

"Unlikely," said Otani with more confidence than he felt. "I think they go on a scale of culmination. This morning's was a fairly lively tremor, this one enormously stronger. As you say, about as strong as they come. If we do have another, goodbye and thanks; but I don't think we will. We'll call the Agency for a situation report in a few minutes, then see what the mess is like outside.''

As the minutes passed the mood of menace seemed to dissipate itself, and Otani began to feel in his bones that the convulsion had indeed been final. The Meteorological Agency's lines were all tied up and the National Police Agency in Tokyo seemed more disposed to ask questions than to give information. It did prove possible to make contact with the seismological laboratory at Suma, and the news was mildly encouraging. The shock had indeed been very severe: Force Seven on the Richter Scale, but preliminary indications were that the epicentre was much further away than that of the tremor in the morning. Its precise location was still to be established, but prospects of avoiding a tidal wave seemed good.

They were all more than a little shaken, and even Noguchi seemed more thoughtful and less detached than usual. In less than half an hour the room had been set roughly to rights and the telephones were all busy again, establishing the extent of damage in the Prefecture. The fire services would go their own way: members of a much more highly regarded profession than the police, with traditions going back to medieval times, firemen tended to take a lofty attitude about being told what to do. Even so, the duty officer at Kobe Fire Headquarters expressed his appreciation of the early warning they had been given, and was forthcoming about the situation as they saw it.

Somewhat surprisingly to the officers of the Fire Brigade, the teeming wooden shacks and doss-houses of the slum areas seemed to have come off very lightly. No serious fires had been reported, and the Brigade had heard that one or two minor outbreaks had been handled quite competently by the local people themselves. It would be an hour or so before they could be sure, but things did not look too bad. The only major blaze within the city limits was in a block of restaurants and shops: the Brigade thought they could contain it. No requests for help had been received from neighbouring fire authorities. Otani decided to wait until later to congratulate Noguchi on the success of his efforts, and sat quietly watching his men systematically collecting situation reports. He was worried about Hanae and the others, but something inhibited him from making a private telephone call before some broad picture of the condition of the millions of citizens in the region had emerged.

It was not long in coming. The quake had taken place at one-twenty-two, and by just after three there were coloured pins in the wall map covering all the divisions under his command, indicating that reports had been received. Kobe City itself had been worst hit, and there was a good deal of structural damage in the second largest city, Himeji, to the west. About as serious as a really bad typhoon in terms of the clearing up to be done, the local man said. An old man had died of a heart attack, and there had been a number of traffic accidents, with some fatalities.

The traffic police throughout the south of the Prefecture reported numerous pile-ups resulting from loss of control by drivers travelling at speed when the shock occurred. They had been expecting a high accident rate on the holiday in any case, but the number of incidents was such that they had not yet been able to log them all. The rural and mountainous areas to the north seemed to have suffered scarcely at all, but the attendant in charge of the tigers in a private zoo attached to a Buddhist temple of all places had left the cage unlocked at feeding-time in his agitation, and a pair of three-year-old animals were now at large in the wooded hills somewhere. Escapes by dangerous animals were a regular feature of life in Otani's enormous domain, and he gave little heed to the report. The real harm was much nearer home.

There had been deaths. Not all that many more than on a normal day, but the damage to property in Kobe was immense. The young woman official to whom Otani had spoken at the Prefectural Government office earlier had by some miracle managed to round up enough colleagues to arrange for ward offices to open up school buildings in badly affected areas to accommodate some hundreds of people rendered at least temporarily homeless until burst water mains could be mended, gas leaks traced and dealt with, and makeshift repairs made to the newer, concrete apartment blocks which fared so much worse than wooden buildings when their foundations bucked and protested under the exceptional stresses.

A good many people had been injured by falling furniture, some of them seriously, and a number of pharmacies and local clinics were opening up to cope with the demand for medication for bruises, cuts and other minor injuries. On top of everything else, local police stations were being besieged with enquiries as cars flooded back into the city, bringing day-trippers back to face whatever chaos had been made of their homes.

"All in all, it's a very grim picture," said Otani to Hanae in conclusion of his own summary when at last he felt able to spare a few minutes to ring her. The gods had been kind to them. Hanae had reached the Shimizus' flat just as they were deciding what to do with their day. They had needed little persuading to go back with her to the house at Rokko, where they were all safe. Moreover, Akira had managed to ring through to a neighbour who did have a telephone and had learned that the block was being evacuated because of a broken water main. They would therefore stay put. There seemed to be no damage at all at Rokko.

"Good," said Otani. "One way and another I suppose things could have been a great deal worse." He rubbed a painful bruise on his shin, reflecting that it must have been inflicted by the heel of Migishima's regulation boot.

I suppose you won't be able to come home yet," said Hanae rather wistfully.

"In a couple of hours, I expect," said Otani. "Inspector Sakamoto has just arrived. He wasn't due to take over as duty officer till six. He's been out of town and came in as quickly as he could." He lowered his voice conspiratorially. "You know what he's like." Sakamoto was on the other side of the room, rigidly correct, and tut-tutting as he straightened a framed certificate of commendation which was askew on the wall. ''Terrible old bore, but marvellous at clearing up messes. He'll come into his own tonight. Ninja has just left to go and see how his friends in the criminal classes are getting on, and I'm going to drive round a bit and form my own impressions of the situation. My own office is impossible to work in—broken glass all over the place. I really don't expect to be late, Ha-chan.''

He put the telephone down and beckoned to Migishima. ''Go and find my driver,'' he said. ''His name's Tomita. He was in here a while ago. Blue zippered jacket. I expect he'll be in the garage, worrying about the car. Tell him to bring it round; I want to drive about the city for a while.'' As Migishima turned away, Otani acted on a curious impulse. ''You can come with me, if you like,'' he said.

Chapter 5

MIGISHIMA HELD THE DOOR OPEN FOR OTANI, CLOSED IT after him with a resounding bang, then climbed stiffly into the front passenger seat. Tomita sniffed audibly in disapproval. "Just cruise round for half an hour or so," Otani instructed him. "Take a swing past the Motomachi shopping area where the fire is. And we'll have a look at the business buildings and the harbour. Then out through Nada ward and take me home."

The afternoon was still fine and clear, in spite of the smoke rising from the shopping district a mile or so west, and the perceptible acrid smell of burning in the air. As they approached the normally bustling streets of shops, restaurants and department stores the oddity of the atmosphere became more pronounced. The shuttered holiday appearance of some whole blocks contrasted dramatically with the frenzy of fire-fighting activity nearby. Hoses were snaking from the hydrants, as firemen in their silvery rubberised gear not unlike samurai armour of the middle ages moved on their mysterious errands, and the radio telephone in the command car crackled urgently.

A number of proprietors and managers of shops and restaurants had arrived on the scene and were helping to organise the work of salvage, their casual holiday clothes in incongruous contrast to the grim expressions on their faces: adequate insurance is still deemed by many to be something of an eccentric extravagance. Otani told Tomita to stop, and got out of the car to speak briefly to the officer in charge.

The blaze was under control, but it had been a major outbreak. Five bodies had already been recovered, and there would be more when his men could penetrate to the heart of the fire. Seven people had been taken to hospital with burns and injuries of varying degrees of severity, and the material damage was immense. There would have to be major clearance and rebuilding throughout the block.

Otani nodded grimly and returned the officer's salute. Before setting out he had changed into the uniform he always kept in reserve in the locker in his office, and now looked every inch the senior officer in his grey-blue tunic, highly polished belt and shoes, gold braid and insignia of rank. The car moved on, and into a side street where a water main had been ruptured by the earthquake. Two small boys in their underpants were cavorting in and out of the fountain of water in a solemn intensity of rapture, oblivious to the chaos nearby. Otani felt oddly pleased. It *was* Boys' Day, after all.

A thought struck him. The Shimizus' apartment was no more than ten minutes' drive away. No harm in driving by to form an impression of the external damage, at least. He told Tomita to make the diversion, and the car headed towards the housing development on the edge of the inner city area. He had never used the official car to visit his daughter and her husband; it would have been improper. No need to enlighten the two in front, therefore. Otani gazed at the backs of the two heads in front of him. The tendons in Migishima's neck were clearly visible.

"Relax, Migishima," he said suddenly, then continued to speak without giving him a chance to respond. "Tomita, you should know that Migishima here acted with great presence of mind during the quake. He didn't save my life, but might very well have done, at the expense of his own."

Tomita's own rigid demeanour altered slightly, and he

glanced into the driving mirror dubiously. "Sir?" he said in a cautious voice.

Otani nodded to the reflection in the mirror. "Yes. Well done, Migishima. We'll drop you off near your home if you let Tomita know the best place when we go through Nada." They drove on, and Otani noted with satisfaction that Tomita began to talk to Migishima in an undertone.

There were eight blocks of flats in the Minami development, and it was clear to Otani at first sight that he and Hanae would have company at the house for at least two or three days. The block in which the Shimizus lived had an open crack many metres long down one side, and water was pouring out of the main entrance in a steady stream. Theirs was not the only block affected. Everywhere people were loading belongings into cars, from colour television sets to the pathetic small appurtenances of baby care like plastic pots and piles of nappies. It was a depressing sight.

"Would you do something for me, Migishima?" Otani asked abruptly as they drove slowly past the Shimizus' block. "Stop the car, Tomita, I want to get out for a minute."

Migishima shot out of his seat and wrenched open the door for Otani, who beckoned him back a few paces and pointed up to the roof of the block. Four improvised bamboo flagpoles leant at drunken angles, each bearing a pair of the brightly-coloured carp streamers, now drooping sadly in the still air of later afternoon.

"You see the extra large ones, second from the right?" Migishima nodded in bafflement. "I'd be obliged if you would see if you can get up there and bring that pair down for me. There's an emergency staircase up on to the roof, and it looks as if it's still quite solid." Otani's lips twitched as he saw the incredulity in the young policeman's face, and was tempted to leave him in the dark to see what would happen. Then he relented. "It's all right, officer," he said. "I haven't taken leave of my senses. Those *koi nobori* belong to my small grandson. And my grandson will be staying at my house for a while, so they ought to go up over my rooftop. Off you go."

Migishima beamed with relieved comprehension and

bolted towards the entrance. Otani strolled back to the car and enlightened Tomita, who exhibited toothy pleasure and only the slightest hint of loss of face at not having been given the job himself. What seemed like mere seconds later, Migishima came into view on the rooftop, approached the lopsided flagpole and carefully disentangled the tapes and cords which fastened the bunting to it. He then draped the smaller of the two streamers round his shoulders while he folded the larger one, which was fully eight feet long. The second one in its turn folded, Migishima disappeared again and shortly emerged from the ground-floor entrance flushed with triumph, his trousers soaked to the knee.

Tomita helped him re-fold the streamers with military neatness, and stowed them in the boot of the car. Preoccupied as the people in the vicinity were, a little knot of bystanders assembled as the policemen acted out their tableau, and embarrassment stirred in Otani's heart. Standing with impassive dignity beside the car, he silently upbraided himself as a silly old fool, making two loyal subordinates look clownish and ridiculous for the sake of a stupid sentimental whim of his own, on a day when hundreds were suffering loss, injury and even bereavement.

He climbed back into the car in morose silence and waited for the other two. When they got in he spoke quietly. "I apologise to you both," he said simply. "I have abused my position and yours by asking such a personal favour. Especially as I knew that my family are safe when others are suffering. Drive back to the business area, Tomita, please."

The car moved off, and the silence was heavy for a while. Then Migishima spoke to Tomita, in a voice intended to be overheard. "I have a young brother, and we always take Boys' Day very seriously at home. We fly the same *koi nobori* my parents bought for me when I was a baby. I suppose it must be the Superintendent's grandson's first Boys' Day—the streamers are brand new. It would have been terrible to lose them. I was very glad to recover them." Tomita agreed earnestly, and Otani heaved a deep breath.

"Thank you," he said, then adopted a brisk, peremptory manner. "Right, well, let's get on with it, Tomita."

Their route took them through the industrial belt along the seafront, where the general shutdown of the factories for the holiday week gave the area a dead quietude beyond mere Sunday calm. Most of the buildings were of one or two storeys, and the only damage which was obvious was a wrecked corrugated-iron roof on which a brick chimney had collapsed. Lumps of brickwork were scattered over the road, and Tomita skirted them fastidiously after waiting for a car coming from the opposite direction to negotiate the same stretch. "Lucky it's holiday week, sir," he observed. "Hardly any work going on. Except the *sake* brewery, of course; can't shut that down."

Otani was feeling better, and nodded almost affably. "The shock will have stirred up the mash," he said. "The next batch of Hakutsuru Brand will be either specially good or very doubtful." The unearthly silence persisted as they approached the office blocks of the trading companies near the harbour. This was the first part of Kobe to be developed in the nineteenth century, and there was a spacious, confident style to its planning, even though the first generation of wood and brickbuilt godowns and offices had long since given way to the modern container stores and loading bays with adjoining office blocks of concrete and glass.

The sun was low in the western sky and when they reached the seafront there was a golden quality in the light. The windows of the car were open, and Otani cocked an ear. "Stop the car," he said. "Switch off the engine. There's a dog howling somewhere over there." All three men got out of the car and stood for a moment in the freshness, the smell of the sea all about them. A light breeze was coming inshore, and it was beginning to feel chilly. There was a tranquillity about the place in spite of the broken glass littered about and the dismal baying which sounded quite near, though it was muffled and obviously emanating from behind closed doors.

They were standing in a sizable open space, roughly rectangular in shape. One side was made up of moorings, open to the sea. Two lighters were made fast. One was empty, the other fully laden with its load covered with securely lashed tarpaulins. A small but powerful looking mobile crane stood at one end of its miniature railway track. The westward side was sealed off by a high boundary fence made of concrete beams, while to the east the boundary was marked by the approach road down which they had driven.

The main buildings on the side opposite the moorings consisted of a warehouse of modern construction and beside it what was evidently an administrative and office block, of three storeys. It was from this building that the broken glass had come, and above which a large roof-mounted display sign now hung at an angle, one of its supporting brackets having come adrift. The lettering was in Roman script.

Hockmuth-Wassermann K.K.

Otani neither spoke nor read English or any other European language, although he had been made to learn the alphabet as a schoolboy. During his brief career in Imperial Naval Intelligence in the last stages of the war he had been assigned to a crash course in Russian and could still remember a few words and phrases, but had years before concluded that he was no linguist. He looked up at the sign. The letters "K.K.", the initial shorthand for "Limited Company", were to be seen everywhere in modern Japan. The other words must be names of some kind.

"Can you read it?" Otani asked. The younger generation were much better at this sort of thing. "Is it names, or what they deal in?"

"Names, sir," said Migishima smartly. *"Hokumuto-Basaman.* German, I think."

"We must do something about that wretched dog," said Otani, moving forward. "What makes you think it's German?"

"I studied German in college, sir," Migishima replied. "Their family names are very much like ours—that is, they often have a meaning in ordinary language. I recognise those two. You could call them Pride and Waterman in Japanese."

Otani gave a snort of derision as they crunched over slivers of broken glass. "Ridiculous," he said briefly, then turned to Tomita who was waiting by the car. "You'd better get on the radio, Tomita," he called. "Let the duty room know where we are. Tell them I'll be on my way home very shortly. Now, Migishima, are you any use with dogs? If this one has been shut up for days on end it may be savage."

Migishima gulped. "I don't like them much," he confessed.

Otani looked him up and down. It was as well that this young paragon had some chinks in his armour. "Very well, I'll lead the way. It won't be difficult to get in." He nodded at the gaping hole left by the shattering of a panel of glass by the closed main entrance. The dog seemed to be shut in a room somewhere upstairs, and the persistent howling had a disturbing quality.

Otani ducked carefully through the jagged hole and Migishima followed. They found themselves in a small, severely functional reception area. A plain desk faced them in the space beside the stairway, with two hard upright chairs opposite. Beyond a partition on the other side was what looked like a general office, containing three desks and the usual paraphernalia of filing-cabinets, typewriters, yellowing notices pinned or taped to the wall, and two calendars which still showed April. An old-fashioned wooden coatrack had toppled over and was leaning crazily against a desk with a blue beret and a badly-furled umbrella hanging out unnaturally from it. A wire basket which must have been balanced too near the edge of a desk had fallen to the floor, releasing a scatter of papers. There was an unpleasant smell in the air and Otani paused and sniffed.

"Can you smell anything?" he demanded, and Migishima sniffed too, looking around.

Then the young man pointed. "Stale water from the flower, sir," he said. A narrow-necked vase was lying on its side on one of the desks, a very dead iris crushed against the cover of the typewriter. The smell was indeed coming from a puddle of water on the desk.

Satisfied, Otani turned towards the staircase. The state of the office was much as might have been expected. On an afterthought, he turned back and picked up a telephone which was dangling from its wire, the receiver on the floor. There was a good deal of loose plaster everywhere, and Otani dusted his hands off with a paper handkerchief as he made his way to the stairs. "The telephone people will be having their problems," he remarked. "Wires down, and receivers off the hooks in offices all over the place."

He led the way up the plain concrete staircase which was cracked here and there but basically intact. Apart from the non-slip metal and rubber edgings on each tread, the concrete was unsoftened by any form of covering. This made the contrast with the second flight all the greater. The landing was close-carpeted, and the stairs above almost opulent; the walls were panelled with good quality walnut veneer. The second landing was quite spacious, with two doors leading off, the staircase continuing up beyond. The racket made by the dog was coming from behind the door immediately facing Otani. The animal was in a room which must have a view over the seafront, but the glass in the windows was evidently intact or the dog might very well have jumped out to freedom.

Otani paused at the head of the stairs and waited for Migishima. Then, feeling rather foolish, he drew his regulation pistol from its holster and moved towards the door. If the creature were crazed with hunger and thirst it might well attack, and it would be stupid to take unnecessary risks. "I'm going to try the door. If it's unlocked I shall open it just a fraction. Not enough for the dog to get through. Then we'll see what happens."

The dog must have heard his voice, for the howling stopped abruptly. The ensuing silence was if anything even more unnerving, and Otani felt a distinct uneasiness as he stretched out his left hand and twisted the ornate brass door-knob. The door was unlocked, and opened inwards. Otani eased it forward, fully prepared to see slavering fangs at the other side of the crack. Nothing happened, so he pushed the door a little wider, ready to slam it shut again immediately if necessary. The best light of the day was gone and it was gloomy on the landing, but it was much brighter inside the room, and the Persian carpet on the floor inside struck the eye with its rich reds and blues.

Now the dog inside began to whimper, but quietly now. It

sounded some way from the door, so Otani very cautiously drew close to the crack and opened the door wide enough to take a quick look inside. What he saw made him fling the door wide open and go in, quite forgetting Migishima behind him.

The room was of a comfortable size but far from large. It put Otani somewhat in mind of Professor Horiguchi's study in the house at Miyazu. This was because of the carpet, the glass-fronted bookshelves in dark wood and the big, old-fashioned desk. Apart from this it was unmistakably an office. On the desk was a dictating machine, the red indicator light on the hand microphone glowing like a jewel. There was a grey metal filing-cabinet with a combination lock in a corner of the room, and a metal notice-board on the wall beside the door, with flow-charts and other papers held to it by magnetic discs like the black stones in a game of *go.* On a side table was a full-sized electric typewriter with a sheet of paper in it, and on another was a silver tray laden with bottles of whisky, gin, brandy and other more exotic liquors.

The dog's evident distress was not on account of hunger or thirst, it would seem. On sheets of newspaper spread on the carpet was a bowl about a third full of water, and another containing some kind of biscuit-like food. Otani had never kept a dog, but one of his neighbours had a big black one like this glossy creature so he was able to identify it as a Labrador. It continued to moan and whimper, but not menacingly, and Otani slowly returned his pistol to the leather holster on his belt as he looked at the slumped figure of the man before him.

He became aware of Migishima at his side, but said nothing until he had carefully circled the desk, his eyes fixed on the still figure. When he tentatively reached out a hand, the Labrador growled with an instant reaction, and Otani hastily drew back. Then he looked at Migishima, who had an expression of absorbed fascination on his face. "There is no movement," he said. "No indication of breathing; but we must check, and I don't think the dog will allow anyone to touch him. Go and ask Tomita to radio for a dog-handler to be sent urgently."

"And an ambulance, sir?" said Migishima as he made for the door.

"Not yet," said Otani. "The ambulance service have enough on their hands, and I don't somehow think there will be any particular urgency about moving this man."

Migishima disappeared, and Otani resumed his scrutiny of the figure at the desk. Even though his face was concealed from view, the man was obviously not Japanese. He was in shirtsleeves, the cuffs secured by heavy gold links. He must have been getting on in years; the freckled bald head was fringed with sparse grey hair, and the skin at the back of the neck coarse and pitted. Otani looked round for a jacket, and saw it on a hanger behind the door. He crossed to it, but the dog again snarled threateningly as he extended a hand to it. Confound the creature; it would be some time before a dog-handler could arrive, but Otani could scarcely bring himself to shoot the handsome beast for the sake of half an hour. He would have to wait it out, or pacify the dog somehow.

The Labrador had taken up its vigil at its master's right, between the side of the big desk and the door, and Otani now went to the window. He could see his car below, and make out the burly young figure of Migishima talking into the radio handset. Oddly there was no sign of Tomita, and Otani wondered where he was. His puzzlement was short-lived, because the driver now appeared at the door of the room.

"I apologise for the intrusion, sir," he said awkwardly. "I should have spoken earlier, when we heard the howling. But I have had quite a lot to do with dogs. I wonder if perhaps I could try to help . . ." Without waiting for a reply Tomita approached the whimpering animal, crooning softly in a kind of gentle gibberish as he did so; and to Otani's surprise he did seem to have a soothing effect on it. Still wearing his cheap and garish jerkin and vulgar shoes, and being in any case an unremarkable looking little man, Tomita cut an incongruous figure as he boldly reached out a hand to the big dog, still uttering his oddly pleasant but meaningless sounds; but the animal submitted itself to being patted and stroked.

Tomita squatted on his haunches and continued to fondle and talk to the dog, breaking off briefly to look up at Otani.

"You could examine the man now," he said almost off-handedly, then returned his attention to the Labrador. A little dubiously, Otani reached out and tried to find a pulse in the wrist nearest to him. Tomita was right; the dog did not react. Nor did the slumped figure at the desk. There was no trace of a pulse, and Otani now boldly pulled the arm clear of the face.

The staring grey eyes were enough to proclaim that the man was dead, but there was no obvious wound or other sign to indicate what had befallen him. The body was still warm, but the heavy, jowly face had the waxy appearance that Otani had seen too often in the course of his career to leave him in any doubt. He crossed to the jacket on its hanger behind the door. In the breast pocket was a clean folded handkerchief, which Otani shook out and placed lightly over the dead man's face. The dog had been quite enough until Tomita had pacified it: they could do without a fixed glare from a corpse.

Otani heard the clump of boots on the concrete stairs below. "That will be Migishima," he said to Tomita. "Do you think you could get the dog out of the building? We can't leave it here."

The Labrador was wearing a massive leather collar, and Tomita examined it. There was a heavy metal ring to take a leash, and he glanced round the room. "It would be simpler with a leash, sir, but I don't see one in the room."

Otani looked round as well. "It's here," he said after a moment. The plaited leather leash was hanging behind the jacket, and Otani handed it over and watched Tomita attach it to the dog's collar, still murmuring reassuringly.

Migishima had arrived at the door, and put a prudent distance between them as Tomita led the dog out, patting it as they went. "Well done," said Otani with feeling as he watched them disappear. "We'll decide later what to do with him." He turned to Migishima. "Right. We'll go through his pockets, though I doubt if we shall have any trouble identifying him. This is obviously his office."

The jacket was well tailored, and bore the name of a Hong Kong maker. The outer pockets yielded a set of car keys, some loose change and a leather clip for paper money. "Write it down, Migishima,'' Otani said. ''Twenty-seven thousand five hundred yen in notes, plus four hundred and . . . eighty in coins.'' From the inside breast pocket he produced a bulky wallet and three letters. One was a printed air-letter form, creased and tattered, one bore a Japanese stamp and was addressed in Japanese, while the third was in a crisp foolscap envelope with an airmail sticker and a foreign stamp.

Otani set them on one side and opened the wallet. The alien's registration card he expected to find was inside and the photograph on it was of the dead man. His name was given in phonetic Japanese script as well as Roman letters and was therefore as easy for Otani to read as the address. ''*Richiyado Riibaman,*'' he read aloud. ''Lives in Nishinomiya.'' He delved further into the wallet. ''Here's one of his name-cards.'' He glanced at it and handed it to Migishima, who with a touch of pride turned it over and read the non-Japanese side.

RICHARD LIEBERMANN
Managing Director
Hochmuth-Wassermann & Co (Japan)

In one corner was the office address, and in another that of a house in the most expensive part of suburban Nishinomiya, between Kobe and Osaka.

Otani looked at Migishima. ''Well, officer, you've just completed your training. What are the correct procedures to be followed now?'' A deep flush suffused the young man's face. It was dusk outside and becoming difficult to see inside the room, but Otani made no move to switch on the lights.

''Sir,'' said Migishima, and paused. ''Sir, if we are satisfied that the man is dead, it is necessary to consider whether there are any suspicious circumstances. This will entail making a preliminary judgment about the cause of death.''

Otani nodded. ''Correct. Well, go and have a look. Put the lights on first.''

Migishima gulped audibly, and went over to the light switch. He hesitated, then pressed it. Nothing happened.

"The earthquake must have cut off the current," he said with relief.

"No," said Otani curtly, and pointed to the ruby glow of the indicator light on the dictating machine. "The ceiling fitment may have been broken. Try the desk lamp."

Migishima went to the desk, and light sprang from the low-powered lamp in the Anglepoise fitment, making the bald head glisten as Migishima reached out and gingerly removed the handkerchief. "Heart attack, sir?" he said hopefully.

"Possibly," said Otani, then took pity on the boy. "Come, we shall have to straighten him up," he said. "I've only seen the face and tried for a pulse so far." He went to the desk himself and they each lifted one shoulder, tipping the man backwards in his big executive swivel chair.

The fixed, unseeing eyes now pointed at the ceiling, and Otani replaced the handkerchief. There was still no sign of a wound or other injury, and Otani shook his head. "I don't know," he said thoughtfully. "There *have* been reports of deaths from heart attacks today. It was a very severe quake, and such occurrences aren't all that uncommon. You may be right. Well, what next?"

Migishima closed his eyes as if about to recite a poem in school. "Notify the family . . . and of course, he's a foreigner. Also the German Consul. At least, I suppose he is German."

Otani looked again at the alien's registration card on the desk. "Yes, he is. It says so here. Good. You're keeping your head. So no suspicious circumstances, in your opinion? Don't you find it a little odd that a wealthy foreign businessman comes to work on a public holiday, bringing his dog and the animal's food with him? But no staff, no secretary, the place deserted?"

Otani paced about restlessly, crossing to the window, then to the door. Migishima put on a mulish expression. "With respect, sir, I don't see why not. He might have thought it a good chance to catch up with his work in peace and quiet. The holiday isn't particularly significant to a foreigner."

"True," Otani agreed. He stopped, and wheeled round.

"Better switch off that dictating machine. How far had he got?"

Migishima looked at the machine, which was of the type that records on a flexible plastic sheet. "He couldn't have begun, sir," he said. "There's nothing in the machine."

Otani crossed to the desk and looked for himself, but said nothing. Then he rubbed a hand over his chin. "Keys. Car keys in his pocket, but no car outside. How did he get here?" He stood indecisively for a moment, then crossed again to the window. There were two heavy lorries parked by the loading bay, obviously left there over the holidays. Tomita was visible in the dusk, half in and half out of the driving seat of the black and white police car, its door wide open. He was still apparently talking to the dog, which was now stretched out beside the car. There were no other vehicles in the vicinity.

"I'm not happy," he said at last. "Find a big envelope, if you can." Migishima tried the desk drawers, two of which were locked. In one of the others was a quantity of stationery, including some large manila business envelopes with the name of the firm printed on them in English and Japanese. Otani watched him produce one. "Good. Put all that stuff from his jacket into it, and seal it. No, wait a minute." He approached the dead man and felt the area of the pockets of the trousers stretched over the pudgy thighs, concluding with some relief that they were empty. It would have seemed oddly obscene to have had to delve into them. He nodded to Migishima to seal the envelope, then took from his own pocket his personal seal in its little leather case. Opening it, he took out the small cylindrical block of ivory with the Chinese characters of his surname carved in relief in a circular border at one end. The case incorporated a tiny red inkpad on which he pressed the seal before printing its impression across the join of the envelope flaps at each end.

"Bring it with you," he said to Migishima. "Turn off the light, and come with me." There was a key in the lock on the inside of the door, and Otani transferred this to the outside, locking the door on the body as they left. It was now very dark on the stairs, and not easy to negotiate the broken glass at the entrance. The heavy door was locked, however, and Otani wasted no time in looking for a key.

Migishima sniffed the fresh sea air outside with deep relief. "May I ask the Superintendent what he intends to do?" he enquired with stilted formality.

Otani's facial expression was unreadable in the gloom. "You may ask the Superintendent by all means," he replied amiably. "To be frank, the Superintendent isn't too sure. At the very least, we shall now have to send for an ambulance and have the body removed to the mortuary. Then, stretched as we are today, we shall nevertheless have to arrange for a man to be posted here overnight. I want an autopsy, and I want that office room sealed with everything in it until we have the result. Inspector Sakamoto can take care of notifying the family, and the German Consul can wait till morning. It isn't every day we have a bad earthquake to contend with, and I'm as tired as I'm sure you must be, young man."

They reached the car, and Otani gazed down at the dog. "I compliment you on your technique, Tomita," he said heavily, beginning to realise just how exhausted he was. "Can you make the dog comfortable somewhere in the garage at Headquarters overnight? Would he be better off with our police Alsatians?"

Tomita did his best to conceal his horror at the suggestion. "I'll take care of him, sir," he said. "The Alsatians would go for him."

Otani flapped a hand wearily. "Whatever you say. I leave it to you. You'd better sit in the back with me, Migishima, then Tomita can have the dog in front. I'll talk to Inspector Sakamoto on the radio first."

Forty minutes later Tomita stopped the car at a junction in Nada ward and Migishima prepared to get out. An ambulance had been and gone, bearing the body of Richard Liebermann to the mortuary at the municipal hospital, and the key of his office was back in Otani's pocket. A policeman equipped with a two-way radio was on duty outside the premises of Hochmuth-Wassermann K.K., and the big Labrador was sound asleep on the front passenger seat beside Tomita.

"You've done well today, Migishima. I hope you have

learned something, too. Have you worked out what the suspicious circumstances are yet?''

Migishima shook his head. "I'm sorry, sir, I still think it would be reasonable to presume that he died of a heart attack caused by the shock of the earthquake.''

Otani opened his eyes wide and stared at the young man. "The earthquake was a very violent one, Migishima. It shattered the heavy glass at the main entrance to the building, and shook the display sign from its fixings. It probably wrecked the ceiling light in his office. But it didn't spill any of the water in the dog's bowl, and it didn't upset any of the bottles on the tray. I think that this was because the water was put there on that perfectly clean newspaper *after* the quake, and that the bottles *had* been toppled over. He simply tidied them up afterwards, and put two broken glasses in the waste-paper basket; I saw them there. A tidy-minded man. I don't think he then sat quietly down and switched on his dictaphone and after that proceeded to have a heart attack. I don't know how he died. We shall try to find out. Goodnight, officer.''

Migishima got out of the car and saluted. "Thank you for the ride, sir. And for permitting me to accompany you. Sir, it could still have been a heart attack. Delayed shock.''

"You are a very obstinate young man," said Otani, "but you may be right, of course. Let's go, Tomita." Tomita let in the clutch and the car slid forward. The back of his neck was again eloquent, and Otani sighed.

"I don't think he meant to be impertinent, Tomita," he said. "It has been quite a day for us all. I am especially grateful to you. I had no idea you had such a way with dogs.''

Mollified, Tomita allowed his shoulders to relax into a more normal posture. "He's a fine animal, sir," he said enthusiastically. "If he looks like needing a new home, we could always keep him at Headquarters. Will you need some help putting up the carp streamers?''

"I'd forgotten all about them," Otani admitted. "Thanks, but we'll manage. It's too dark tonight, and anyway, it's a job for my son-in-law." He relapsed into silence, and Tomita knew him well enough not to break it during the rest of the drive home. In fact, Otani was irritated by the reflection that he and Migishima might very possibly have obliterated a murderer's footprints on the carpeted stairs. The earthquake had left them helpfully dusty. Then there had been that car that had passed them near the *sake* brewery: he couldn't even remember what colour it had been. He shook his head in exasperation. He must be getting old. Like the dead man. Old, heavily built, and living somewhere between Osaka and Kobe. That was what the boy had told Noguchi.

Chapter 6

THE GENERAL SENSE OF CHAOS CAUSED BY THE EARTH-quake all over the Kobe area and the particular disruption brought to the Otani household by the presence of the Shimizus and the baby led to a mood of indecision on Otani's part when he got up the next morning. The weather was still serenely sunny and it took a few minutes for the full recollection of the events of Boys' Day to establish itself in his consciousness. In the few minutes before he went downstairs to join in the unaccustomed bustle of a family Sunday breakfast he wondered if he had gone too far in confiding to the raw young constable his first thought about the dead man they had stumbled upon. Perhaps the excitement of the earthquake had gone to his head, and he had imagined sinister overtones in a perfectly straightforward situation. It could have been as Migishima suggested, and he could be making a quite unnecessary fuss over the death of one man on a day when dozens of other lives had ended, to figure as simple statistics from a police point of view. The idea that there might be a connection with the business of the boy and the gun was probably pure fantasy on his part.

Nevertheless, the man *was* a foreigner, and officialdom demanded that special procedures should be followed. It was an obvious job for Kimura, and the sooner he got on with it the better. Headquarters would be at sixes and sevens however much Inspector Sakamoto might have achieved in the clearing-up process the previous evening, and they would not be at normal working strength till the following day. Otani continued to ponder various courses of action over breakfast, his pensiveness unnoticed in the cheery turmoil generated by others. Akiko and her husband went off early to survey the state of their flat, leaving Hanae to fuss delightedly over the baby; and after they had gone Otani made his way unobtrusively to the telephone and rang the duty officer.

Yes, there was a note on file of what was believed to be Inspector Kimura's latest home telephone number, and it was thought that he had been due to arrive back from vacation the previous evening. Otani considered ringing him direct, and then instructed the duty officer to do so, with a request that Kimura should make contact as soon as convenient. From time to time Otani speculated a little enviously about Kimura's domestic life, and on this occasion thought that if he was going to be interrupted in the middle of some orgiastic endeavour it should be by an anonymous colleague rather than by his commanding officer.

It was soon after eight-thirty when Otani left his instructions, and Kimura did not in fact ring until nearly ten, by which time Otani was becoming thoroughly bored. Pushed firmly to the sidelines by Hanae in the interests of the baby, he sat in the morning sunshine on the wooden step overlooking their small moss garden and leafed through the morning edition of the *Kobe Shimbun*. A display announcement on the front page claimed with smug pride that a bumper number of copies had been printed thanks to the exceptional diligence of the technical staff, notwithstanding a good deal of damage to plant and equipment caused by the tremor. There was a short but thoughtful leading article praising the efforts of the emergency services, and Otani smiled grimly when he read a statement issued by the Vice-Governor from the Imperial Hotel in Tokyo, regretting the Governor's absence on official business in Hawaii and noting with satisfaction that the

61

citizenry of Hyogo Prefecture were well served by the local authorities, even on a major public holiday.

The tally of death and destruction reported by the paper was much as the reports from his own divisional commanders the previous afternoon had suggested, and Otani was glad that so far as he could see there was no mention of the death of a foreign businessman, from a heart attack or any other cause.

When Kimura did at last ring, he seemed to be in high spirits following his disreputable week in the teahouses and massage parlours of Taiwan, and already in possession of a good deal of garbled information about the finding of Liebermann's body. Otani decided to let the pleasantries wait until later, and set to work to give Kimura an accurate outline of the situation and of his suspicions; and instructed him to go to the Hochmuth-Wassermann offices, first trying to get hold of someone on the staff there. Otani would join him there in an hour.

Otani put the receiver down with a sense of relief, then went in search of Hanae to let her know he was going out. Normally she would have been discreetly curious, but she was much too concerned with the baby to pay much attention to what he said. He had almost finished dressing when Tomita arrived with the car, and Otani was slightly irritated by this excess of zeal. He had been planning to find a taxi, and now had to listen to an effusive account of the condition of the Labrador, in whose company Tomita appeared to have passed the night. This lasted nearly all the way to the harbour and the Hochmuth-Wassermann building, and it was something of a relief to get out of the car and put an end to the driver's infatuated ramblings.

In spite of it being a Sunday, he found Kimura, to his surprise, in the costume and role of a respectable ''salaryman'' which he adopted only rarely and then usually after a sustained barrage of sarcasm from Otani. He was closeted with an elderly Japanese employee of the firm who gave his name as Sakai, chief accountant, and who seemed stunned by the situation. Kimura had also managed to round up a detective constable and a fingerprint man, and Otani unlocked the door of Liebermann's office to let them get to work on it. Leaving the old accountant downstairs, Kimura joined Otani on the second-floor landing and greeted his superior properly, with anxious enquiries about his health and that of his relatives.

"What about you, Kimura-kun?" Otani asked when his turn came. "When did you get back? Any damage to your flat?"

Kimura shrugged. "No problem, chief," he said cheerfully. "I got back late last night. Flights into Osaka were delayed—they had some damage in the control tower. But I made it home, and there was just a little clearing up to do, that's all." He gestured into the room where the two plainclothes men were moving about, his intelligent eyes sparkling like black diamonds. "A little clearing up here, too, I think."

He led Otani into the adjoining room. It was smaller than Liebermann's and less luxuriously though still comfortably furnished, and it had a feminine touch about it. "Whose room is this?" Otani asked.

"It belongs to his secretary," said Kimura. "A Miss Ilse Fischer. German too, of course. I have a staff list here. That old chap Sakai gave it to me. He's the senior Japanese employee. Miss Fischer doesn't work regular hours. Sakai says she averages two or three days a week, depending on the amount of correspondence from Germany. He's already broken the news to Miss Fischer at her apartment, and she's coming in later to send a telex to Germany. I'll see her then."

Otani looked around him. The windows of this room too had survived, and whatever mess might have been left by the earthquake must have been straightened up by Sakai or one of the policemen. Apart from a modern metal desk the room contained only a small filing-cabinet, a wall shelf with a few reference books between ebony bookends in the shape of elephants, and a coffee table with a single easy chair. Sitting in it, Otani reached forward and picked up a colourful foreign magazine, which was the only thing on the table apart from a carved figure from a *noh* play which he thought he recognised as the heavenly being in the feathered robe from *Hagoromo*.

The magazine was printed back to front, of course, and was

full of photographs of European women in absurd high-fashion clothes. Otani leafed through it without much interest before putting it back. It was probably the magazine and the pale green curtains at the window that made it clear the room was normally occupied by a woman. There was also perhaps a hint of perfume in the air. Very likely she kept various pots and powders in her desk drawer, and he briefly toyed with the idea of acquiring a girl clerk. Then he pulled himself together.

"Let's go next door," he said, getting up. "What happened about notifying the family last night?" ·

"Sakamoto left word that he'd drawn a blank," said Kimura as he held the door open for Otani to go through. "There's a telephone number listed in the directory and it seemed to be ringing, but there was no reply. So he sent a patrol car. No answer at the door, and the neighbours busy clearing up after the quake. Old busybody next door said the German couple didn't keep a servant and that Mrs Liebermann was often away. She'd noticed the man go off with his dog during the morning, but said she hadn't seen his wife for some time. Dying of curiosity, she was . . ."

Nothing about foreigners greatly surprised Otani, who regarded them much as creatures from another planet and could never understand Kimura's taste for their company. Nevertheless, it would be almost inconceivable for a Japanese wife to go off on her own and remain a wife for very long. "Children?" he said, and Kimura shook his head.

"None. I checked the residence permit record before I came here," he said. "I thought I'd make contact with the German Consulate General in Osaka after we finish here. There won't be anybody working on a Sunday, but I . . . that is, I know one of the secretaries there quite well . . ." His voice tailed off as Otani shook his head sorrowfully, watching the fingerprint man at work.

Liebermann's office looked less impressive to Otani in broad daylight. He had brought the manila envelope which he had sealed the previous evening, and now put it on the corner of the desk. "I'm sorry," he said to the two plainclothes men, who stood deferentially waiting for permission to carry on. "You might get something useful off the desk and chair, but there were three of us wandering about in here last night. I remember there were two locked drawers in the desk, and then there's that filing-cabinet." He sucked air in through his teeth. "I hesitate to force them open at this stage . . . just make what investigation you can without them for now, and we'll see."

He turned to Kimura. "This is a German company, Inspector. Tell me, would they carry on their business in German?"

Kimura shook his head. "I doubt it. Only correspondence with their head office in Germany and one or two other German firms here. Virtually all the foreign businesses in Japan operate in English, even the French who hate having to. That old man Sakai told me that he and the other office staff have to be able to understand English and that Liebermann handled all the German language work himself, with Miss Fischer of course."

Otani pulled at the lobe of his right ear, pursed his lips and shook his head worriedly. "I know it's Sunday, but still . . . no next of kin informed, no cause of death notified yet, the consular authorities still unaware. We can't blame everything on the earthquake. You'd better get on with some of the formalities while we wait for the autopsy report. We really can't start searching and questioning people unless we've real grounds. If the man did die from natural causes there's no call to interfere, and we should simply hand this envelope over to his legal personal representative. And the dog, of course," he added as an afterthought.

Kimura's eyes flickered round the room and he managed to suppress a smile as he visualised Otani, normally the picture of self-contained dignity, keeping a timidly wary distance as his driver of all people soothed a big black dog. "The sooner we get the autopsy report the better," he agreed, and Otani nodded.

"Until then, we can't decide whether to mount a full-scale investigation or not. You'll have to be careful with the German woman, Kimura-kun. I suppose you'll be able to talk to her in English?"

"She's sure to be able to speak it," Kimura said confidently. "I've never met a German in Japan who couldn't."

"Well, I think I'll leave you to it," said Otani with mingled relief and regret as he stood up. "You'd better just trust your own judgment. It's your case now and I won't get in your way. Sorry to bring you in on a Sunday, but it's been a funny sort of week. Take charge of that envelope, will you? And I think it would be reasonable to insist we get hold of the fellow's wife." He would have given a good deal to force the locked drawers on the off-chance that there might just possibly be photographs of Noguchi's young delinquent and his companions inside. He hovered in the doorway, dithering about leaving. "I wish you luck with this Fischer-san person," he said as Kimura quested about him with tiny movements like those of a bird, willing him to go. "Yes, well, I'll be on my way. Oh, did the overnight man report anything untoward?"

Kimura shook his head. "No. Everything quiet, chief," he said. "Don't worry. I'll keep you in the picture." Otani finally tore himself away and made his way out of the building.

He felt no inclination to put in an appearance at Headquarters. The clearing-up operation wouldn't get fully under way until the next day, and with the appropriate senior officer now in charge of the puzzling business of the German he might as well relax. "Take me home again, please," he said as Tomita held the car door open for him. It might be pleasant to indulge in a little belated Boys' Day observance in the company of his grandson; provided he could extract him from the clutches of Hanae. "And then for heaven's sake go off duty yourself."

Tomita was delighted at the prospect of an early reunion with the Labrador, and drove a good deal faster than was his normal spinsterly custom. Otani was deposited at the house at lunchtime, to find it deserted. Hanae must have taken the baby down to the shops to show him off. His disappointment was short-lived, and he settled down with a bottle of beer in front of the television and watched an interminable discussion between a professor, two housewives and a member of the Lower House about the role of the family in moral education. He felt pleasantly at liberty. With the Governor in Hawaii and his deputy in Tokyo, it was unlikely that anyone would want to get hold of him.

Chapter 7

KIMURA USUALLY ENJOYED INTERVIEWING FOREIGN women, and the younger the better: he liked to feel that he had the knack of putting them at their ease. On the other hand, Miss Ilse Fischer struck even his susceptible spirit as being a strong-minded sort of lady, and he worked hard to be at his most winsome. Like most Japanese he was bad at estimating the ages of adult Europeans, but he had after all devoted a good many years to the study and appreciation of womankind. Miss Fischer impressed him as looking nearer forty than thirty.

Not that she was going to seed: there was anxiety and strain in her face, but the well-dressed woman raising the coffee-cup to her expertly made-up lips obviously took good care of herself. The blond of her hair was certainly natural, but there was a severity about the way she wore it drawn straight back from her face that gave her a schoolmistressy look. Kimura liked a generous bosom in a woman, such as is rarely found among those of his own race, and noted with appreciation the ample if firmly disciplined curves under the soft black woollen dress she wore. The legs too were long, straight and shapely.

The refreshment had been Kimura's idea realised by the

fingerprint man who found jars of instant coffee and Creap powered milk in a cupboard in the general office downstairs and an electric boiling ring for heating up the water. Kimura sipped some himself, aware that he was still failing to overwhelm Miss Fischer with preliminary courtesies.

"It's really great of you to agree to talk with me today, ma'am," he now said, crinkling his eyes in the manner of Paul Newman. "And to allow me to use English?" His control of the rising inflection he noticed in the speech patterns of so many Americans was uncertain, and he sounded startled rather than warmly encouraging as he had intended.

"It makes nothing," said Miss Fischer tightly. "I am well accustomed to speak English." Her voice was her most attractive obvious feature. Exceptionally low and rather husky, it gave Kimura a brief vision of Western promise.

Kimura shrugged as he had seen Yves Montand do it, and cocked an eyebrow at her. "I wish I could master *any* foreign language the way Europeans seem to be able to handle two or three," he said casually.

Miss Fischer seemed untouched by the compliment and certainly in no mood to return it. "What is it you want, please?" she demanded coldly. "What is for police here to do? Mr Sakai has said that you have shut up his office. We must a hundred things. What is going on?"

Spotting the mistakes in her English gave much satisfaction to Kimura, who cowered humorously under the rapid fire of questions, but it was no use. She glared at him, and he straightened up and spoke soberly and cautiously. "I'll try to explain, ma'am," he said. "Frankly speaking, it's a problem for me. You see, it was my boss who actually *found* Mr Liebermann, entirely by accident, because of the dog howling."

"Since you mention, where is the dog?" Her tone was still one of controlled irritation rather than distress, and Kimura noticed that she fidgeted continuously with the catch of her handbag. "We're taking care of it," Kimura reassured her. "We haven't been able to contact Mrs Liebermann yet, to hand it over to her . . . Anyway, my boss is naturally concerned, because in the case of a foreigner there are special rules and procedures to be gone through. We'll be out from under your feet just as soon as the cause of death is confirmed.''

One carefully plucked eyebrow rose a quarter of an inch. ''You are in some doubt? Mr Sakai has said me that it was, ah, heart stop?''

''Heart attack, coronary. Various ways of putting it,'' Kimura contributed helpfully.

''So. This is not a big surprise. He has for years had trouble of the heart. That terrible earthquake . . . he had often to sit down and take one of his pills.''

She paused and Kimura nodded encouragingly. ''It seems very possible,'' he said. ''Do you happen to know the name of his doctor?''

Miss Fischer gave a distracted little wave of the hand. ''The American clinic in Kobe. The one all the foreigners go.''

Again Kimura resisted the temptation to try to charm her, and continued with neutral courtesy. ''It's a problem for me, Miss Fischer,'' he said. ''Frankly speaking, it would be best for me to speak to Mrs Liebermann first. I shall be sorting out the formalities at the German Consulate General in Osaka later, but . . . do you happen to know where she might be?''

She shrugged with an ostentatious unconcern belied by the wariness in her eyes. ''Why should I? I am a *Sekretärin*, not a friend from her.''

Kimura found it hard to credit this. ''I presume you *know* Mrs Liebermann?'' he asked quietly.

The jerk of her smooth head was quite involuntary, but she covered it well. ''Do *you* know the wives from your colleagues?'' she challenged him.

Kimura was nettled by the question, and maintained his air of sweet reason with an effort. He smiled again, and this time Miss Fischer returned it, with a touch of triumph over having scored a point.

''Well, I guess not many,'' Kimura conceded. ''One or two. But it's quite different for us Japanese. Miss Fischer, my work is mostly with the foreign community, and I know how close they are. My impression is that businessmen's wives are very involved in their husbands' work.''

Miss Fischer sniffed, her composure restored. "Not Frau Liebermann," she said firmly. "You can ask the Japanese staff here. They certainly never have seen.''

Kimura needed time to think about this information, which came as a genuine surprise to him. True, he would have been astounded if Mrs Otani had ever put in an appearance at Police Headquarters, but over the years of his routine contacts with foreigners he had noticed how often their wives telephoned, or dropped in at their offices with requests for help and sometimes startlingly peremptory instructions to the Japanese employees.

"I guess it's a question of the language barrier," he suggested to give himself time. "Foreigners need a lot of help to get about and do things here . . ."

"Frau Liebermann speaks quite well Japanese," said Miss Fischer coldly. "All I know is that she is away often."

"And you have no idea when she may be back?"

"None.''

It was all most peculiar, and Kimura concluded that he could do little more until and unless he could interrogate her formally. He could only indirectly ask her about her own movements on the previous day. He stood up. "Well, thanks anyway,'' he said. "I'll try to raise one of the staff of the German Consulate. I'm sure we'll be able to turn everything back to you in a day or two. May I tell them you'll be notifying your head office?"

"Yes,'' she said. "We have much to do." A tear trickled down her cheek, making her grimness crumple, and she fumbled in her bag and found a paper handkerchief.

"I'm sorry,'' said Kimura awkwardly. "It's a distressing time for you. Did you have any damage at home yesterday?"

She dried her eyes and looked up, softer and more feminine in her vulnerability. "What?" she said vaguely. "Oh. No. No, thank you.''

He opened the door and then looked back. Now that he had vacated her desk he half expected her to move to it, but she seemed lost in thought, and another tear had appeared on her cheek. "I'll be in touch again as soon as possible, Miss Fischer," Kimura said. "I asked Sakai-san to give me your home address and telephone number. I hope you don't mind." Miss Fischer gave no sign of having heard him, and after a short conference with his two assistants he made his way up the alleyway to the road to find a taxi. There was no point in going to the Consulate General offices on a Sunday, but there was a chance that Trudy might be at her pleasant little apartment. One might be able to combine business with pleasure for the rest of the day.

Chapter 8

IT WAS SOMETHING OF A RELIEF TO BE BACK IN NORMAL running order with a full staff following the holidays, even though Otani had not slept well. The prospect of having little Kazuo-chan in the house with his parents had been wholly pleasant, but after two nights Otani was already beginning to admit to himself in his heart of hearts that he was getting too old to cope with what seemed to be the continuous sequence of crises associated with the processes of his grandson's adjustment to his physical and human surroundings.

Fortunately the Shimizus' flat had suffered little internal damage, and repairs to the basic structure of the block were already in hand. In a day or so they would decamp from the house at Rokko and Otani would be able to relapse into the more detached and contemplative pleasures associated with being a grandfather. Even Hanae, whom Otani suspected of being ready to die rather than admit to anything but the purest delight in the situation, had rolled over and muttered crossly in her sleep as the thin banshee wail filled the house for what seemed the twentieth time.

Rather blearily, Otani addressed himself again to the written autopsy report on the desk before him. Well, he had been right in disagreeing with that young fellow. Kimura had a

73

murder on his hands. Otani pressed the buzzer on his telephone and the communicating door to the ante-room flew open almost at once. He had expected to see his usual clerk, and glared forbiddingly at the eager features of Constable Migishima.

"What are you doing here?" he demanded. "Where's my regular man?"

Migishima beamed happily. "In hospital, sir," he said. "Broke a leg water-skiing." He paused. "On Lake Biwa," he then added helpfully.

Otani closed his eyes and sighed deeply. "And you volunteered to take his place, I suppose," he said heavily.

"Yes," Migishima agreed. "I explained to the duty officer that I know how to work your telephone."

Otani surveyed the young man, and then rubbed his hand over his face and smiled wearily. "Well, since I personally instructed you, I suppose you do. Very well, Migishima. You may stand in for the usual man until further notice. Please realise, however, that the events of the day before yesterday were highly unusual. The duties of my clerk are routine and simple, and what I shall mostly require of you is to be as inconspicuous as possible. Now please be so good as to see if Inspector Kimura is in his office. Also find out if Inspector Noguchi is about. I should like to see them both here if possible in"—he looked at his watch—"twenty minutes. At eleven-thirty."

Migishima came stiffly to attention, bowed and disappeared, and Otani sat back in his chair, looking unseeing out of the big window with its view of the cranes and derricks of the port. It had been very lively and eventful with all the family gathered under the same roof after supper the previous evening, but now Otani entertained the ignoble thought that it would be pleasanter if he could look forward to one of his normal quiet evenings at home with Hanae, rather than a repetition of the convivial concentration on the baby's performance of various basic functions. He picked up the autopsy report again. Most interesting, really. Ninja would have something to say about it.

Noguchi came into the room a few minutes ahead of Kimura, and grunted his usual off-hand greeting. "Have a seat, Ninja," said Otani, holding out the paper. "Glance over that while we're waiting for Kimura. Have you seen him yet this morning?"

Noguchi shook his head. "I haven't gone looking for him. I doubt if he's improved." He took the autopsy report and lowered his bulk into one of the chairs Otani kept for visitors.

Otani got up from the desk and went over to join him, a small smile on his face at the thought that Kimura would probably say much the same sort of thing about Ninja, though more elegantly. Their barbed remarks to each other were like seven-flavoured spice in an insipid broth, making all the difference.

Kimura entered the room breezily. He was wearing a completely different ensemble from that of the previous day: the dark suit and sober tie had been replaced by beautifully cut sports slacks and a turtleneck sweater which fitted snugly round his lean but well-muscled torso. "Good morning, chief," he said brightly. "Morning, Ninja."

Noguchi peered up at him disbelievingly, like an aged tortoise investigating the sky on emerging from hibernation. "You're beautiful, Kimura," he said glumly. "I wonder you can bear to look at yourself in the mirror."

"Sit down, Kimura-kun," said Otani briskly. "You two can exchange compliments later. Now this is Kimura's case, but I ordered the autopsy so the report came to me first, about half an hour ago. I asked Ninja to join us after I read it, Kimura. I hope you'll agree that it's interesting enough for us all to put our heads together."

Kimura was in fact deeply offended, but there was nothing to be done but put a reasonable face on it. He nodded tersely, extended an elegantly manicured hand and took the paper from Noguchi as he sat down. While he read it, Otani gave Noguchi a brief and economical account of his discovery of Liebermann's body, watching for Kimura to purse his lips or show some other sign of surprise. He was rewarded when Kimura's eyebrows moved upwards and he whistled a tuneless little phrase. Then he passed the paper back to Otani and looked around the room.

"The doctor was a clever fellow to spot it," said Otani, taking his glasses from his breast pocket and putting them on. "All this about atheroma of the coronary arteries, ischaemia and myocardial infarcts would lead most people to put his death down to heart failure without more ado. Here we are though—damage to carotid arterial walls—presumption of external induction of unconsciousness for duration of at least one cardiac cycle."

"Well, I never heard of an earthquake strangling a man before," said Kimura.

"Not strangling," Noguchi growled. "Not the same thing at all. Nothing about damage to the windpipe. Carotid arteries, it says." Otani continued to scrutinise the report.

"All right, Ninja, if you say so," said Kimura airily. "Surely it amounts to much the same thing?"

Noguchi shook his massive head slowly. "Be your age," he said. "Why would it say it amounted to induced heart failure if the man had been strangled? If he had, the bruises would have stuck out a mile for any idiot to see. Even you would have spotted them."

Otani glanced up over the top of his glasses. It was unusual for Noguchi to be quite so rude to Kimura. "Very well then, Ninja," he said mildly. "How would *you* cut off the blood supply in the carotid artery without strangling the person into the bargain?"

"I'm working it out," said Noguchi, and surprised them both by heaving himself to his feet. "Stand up, Kimura," he commanded peremptorily. He turned to Otani. "What was he wearing?" he asked, as Kimura hesitated, then rose to his feet with evident reluctance.

"Shirtsleeves. No jacket," Otani replied.

"Tie?"

Otani reflected, seeing again in his mind's eye the dead, staring face as he and Migishima hauled Liebermann up from the desk. "Yes," he confirmed.

"No problem if there'd been a jacket," muttered Noguchi as if to himself. Then he moved behind Kimura and with astonishing speed locked one massive forearm round the younger man's neck, simultaneously bringing his left arm up in a chopping movement under Kimura's own left armpit. Kimura's reflexes were fast and he tried to counter, but he was no match for Noguchi. His eyes popping, he was briefly helpless. Then Noguchi released him just as quickly and slumped back into his chair.

Kimura stood in a dazed fury, breathing with some difficulty as he straightened his wrinkled sweater. Gingerly he sat down again and opened his mouth to tell Noguchi what he thought of him. Noguchi forestalled him, speaking with unusual courtesy. "I'm sorry, Kimura-kun," he said, using the friendly suffix he hardly ever bothered with. "I probably shouldn't have done that. But if you'd known it was coming I couldn't have tried it out properly."

Otani nodded thoughtfully, privately relieved that Noguchi had sufficient respect for seniority to have resisted what must have been a temptation to demonstrate on him. "Your counter was pretty fast, Kimura-kun," he said to help the situation. "You obviously got plenty of exercise in Taiwan."

Kimura had regained his normal composure and now looked loftily at Noguchi. "I haven't bothered to take my judo beyond the third *dan*," he said. "That was a flashy sort of trick, but you couldn't have done it if I'd been sitting at a desk."

Like all policemen, Otani had been trained in judo in his day, but had long since abandoned it. He now looked in some awe at Noguchi. "Have you kept it up, Ninja?" he enquired.

Noguchi shook his head and emitted a rumble of what might have been laughter. "Of course not. Kimura could make a monkey of me any time he likes on the mat," he said. "Kimura's good. True, there are plenty of black belts about, but to get to the third *dan* you need class. I never had that, even before I got fat."

His ego thoroughly massaged, Kimura was now all good humour again. "I begin to see the way you're thinking, Ninja," he said. "The bar choke hold might do it, especially with a man of his age taken by surprise. It would be much easier with loose clothing like a jacket to use, though. A tie wouldn't be any good. That *would* bruise the windpipe."

Otani had enough residual knowledge to contribute to the

conversation. "Very well," he said. "Ninja obviously knows about holds and aggressive techniques, and you're the all-round judo expert, Kimura-kun. Given that Liebermann was killed at his desk, how could even an expert do it? Assuming we could show that much, it might tell us most of what we need to know. There can't be many people about who'd be capable. If we're to believe this report it's obviously theoretically possible, or the German wouldn't be dead.''

All three relapsed into silence. Kimura, his eyes closed, twisted his empty hands this way and that experimentally, while Noguchi sat motionlessly mountainous as he brooded. It was Otani who spoke first. "Well, gentlemen," he said, "it's a technical problem which ought to have a technical solution. I'd be grateful if you'd work on it between you. You could turn it over to the judo instructor if you like, or it might be better if one of you went to see the people at the Prefectural Police Training College. No need to advertise our ideas unnecessarily.''

He turned to Kimura. "Let's change the subject," he said. "Tell us what happened at the German Consulate General.''

Kimura's eyes lost the dreamy look they had taken on, as he shifted mental gear and made his report. "I haven't been there," he said. "It was closed yesterday, but I got in touch with one of the staff at home and then they sent a Vice-Consul down to the mortuary with me to do the formal identification, since there's still no sign of the wife.'' He smirked a little self-consciously. "It was another girl I know quite well, actually . . . Miss Beck. It couldn't have been very pleasant for her, especially as they'd obviously been cutting him up by then. I'm surprised they gave her a job like that. Anyway she didn't turn a hair; just identified him and said they'd try to contact Mrs Liebermann. Needless to say, I kept quiet about your suspicions, chief.''

Otani reflected that there was really very little point in trying to be tactful with Kimura. His natural bounce and his excessive quota of self-esteem ensured that he would rarely regard himself as having lost face for very long at a time. Perhaps Noguchi should have squeezed slightly tighter. "Right.

So you took one of your numerous lady friends to the mortuary,'' he said briskly. "Did you have another rendezvous with her this morning?"

Kimura looked wounded. "Of course not," he protested. "I've been here, checking my own records on Liebermann and his wife. And Miss Fischer. I talked to her yesterday too. I've been waiting for this autopsy report to begin organising things properly," he added pointedly.

Otani nodded judiciously. "Good. You'll need all the background information you can come by. What do we know about them already?"

Kimura's heart began to sink. It really would be intolerable if the Old Man proposed to give him the case with one hand and take it away again with the other; and bring Ninja into it quite unnecessarily into the bargain. "I'll send the dossier up for you to see, if you like," he said grudgingly and with a sour glance in Noguchi's direction. Noguchi stirred in his chair but said nothing, and Kimura heaved a little sigh and continued.

"I have very little on any of them," he admitted. "Liebermann arrived here five years ago on a business visa, accompanied by his wife Irmgard. A big age difference. He would have been fifty-eight next month; she's thirty-four. No children, as we already knew. It seems that he was transferred from the Hong Kong office of the Hochmuth-Wassermann firm. His set-up here is quite modest, as you've seen. Well, it seems that Liebermann kept his nose completely clean as far as we're concerned. Papers in meticulous order, residence permit always renewed on time. In fact nothing untoward whatsoever—until now."

"And Fischer-san?"

"Yes, well, I met her yesterday, after you left. I have a copy of her work permit application in my files. She's a bit younger than Liebermann's wife. Thirty-two. I was quite surprised: she looked older to me. She arrived two years ago. There hadn't been approval for the employment of a second German national before, but the Ministry of Justice doesn't seem to have made any difficulties. I expect the business was growing."

"What is the firm's business?" enquired Otani. "I noticed the warehouse, of course."

"Bearings," said Kimura. "Precision bearings. Not very bulky, but extremely heavy in proportion to their size. I was asking the accountant about it yesterday. It struck me that a firm like that would find it economic to switch to air freight for most purposes nowadays, but he said their shipments virtually all come by sea, because of the weight factor. When they get a very specialised order it's despatched by air from Germany, of course. Most of their business is well established, though, and the time-scale for ordering makes sea freight quite feasible."

Otani switched the subject back again. "Well, all that can be gone into later if necessary," he said. "What did this German lady vice-consul have to say about the situation?"

"Well, there wasn't a great deal she *could* say at that stage. I was interested that she didn't seem too surprised to hear that Mrs Liebermann is away somewhere. We talked a bit about the practicalities and Miss Beck thought there'd be no question of sending the body to Germany. The Consulate General will have to sort that out when they talk to the widow." He paused. Otani had taken off his glasses and was tapping them lightly on the autopsy report which he still had on his knee.

"Another odd remark, now I think about it," Kimura went on slowly. "On the way back from the mortuary, Miss Beck asked me what Mrs Liebermann's residence status would be if she wanted to remain in Japan. I told her that of course she could stay for any reasonable period to clear up their arrangements here, but if she wanted to stay on indefinitely the case would have to be taken up with the Immigration Bureau at the Ministry of Justice."

"Yes it would," Otani agreed. "It seems a strange idea, though. We shall have to get hold of this woman soon. I wonder where she can be?" He stood up. "Well it's your case, Kimura-kun. In view of this confirmation of my doubts you'll have to go into full swing. You'll need help with the interviews and statements . . . I'll send a note to Sakamoto to detach a couple of his men to your section for the time being. You'd better straighten things out with the Foreign Ministry

Liaison Office in Osaka too. They'll be upset that you contacted the Germans first, but never mind . . . Oh, keep an eye open for funny business on the financial side at the company. That sort of thing. Interesting case . . . I envy you," he said with a touch of regret, then hastily made a reassuring gesture. "Don't worry, Kimura-kun, I'll try not to interfere. Keep me informed, though. There are three questions, and when you get the answers to each of them, tell me."

He raised a hand and ticked off three fingers. "One, how it was done. Something you'll discuss with Ninja, here. Two, who did it. Three, why." He smiled grimly. "It shouldn't take a clever fellow like you long to find out the answers, Kimura-kun." He nodded in dismissal and walked towards the door with them. "By the way," he said as they left, "don't forget your lad with the gun, Ninja. It occurred to me that Liebermann might just possibly fit the description of the foreigner involved."

It was the last straw for Kimura, who realised that there was now no way he could stop Noguchi from mooching along behind him all the way back to his office. It was perfectly ridiculous to suppose that the respectable Herr Liebermann might be the foreigner they had been trying to track down.

Chapter 9

AKIRA SHIMIZU STOPPED IN HIS TRACKS AND LOOKED AT his father-in-law with interest. They had just left the rice and *sake* shop in a back street near the little covered market by Rokko Station, and each was carrying a large bottle. Shimizu was in his neat office clothes and carried a black document case in his other hand; but having arrived home a full hour earlier Otani had already bathed and changed into the light kimono he always preferred to wear in the evening.

With the baby still the centre of attraction, Otani had been at something of a loose end after his bath, and Hanae must have sensed it. "It's a beautiful warm evening," she said. "Why don't you stroll down to the shops? We need some more *sake*, especially as it's our last family evening for a while."

Otani enjoyed the leisurely walk, with the occasional friendly nods and greetings from neighbours and a particularly respectful salute from the patrolman on duty at the open door of the police box. It was as though the earthquake had discharged psychological as well as seismic tensions, and the mild air of late spring felt amiable and peaceful, like the expressions on the faces of the people about. It had been a pleasant and quite unexpected bonus to spot his son-in-law among a little knot of commuters emerging from the station a minute or two after the inter-urban train from Osaka stopped there.

Shimizu seemed pleased too, and readily accepted Otani's suggestion that they might split a bottle of beer in the tiny refreshment bar beside the station before buying the *sake* and walking up the hill to the house. It was only after a desultory conversation about the effects of the earthquake in Osaka and the prospects for the next round of sumo wrestling championships that Otani mentioned casually that the death of a foreign businessman on the day of the disaster had generated quite a flurry of activity, and by then they had finished the beer and bought the *sake*, not without a mild argument about paying. In the end, Otani let Shimizu buy a second bottle. They might need it for the four of them.

"And all that happened on Boys' Day?" Shimizu said incredulously. "Why didn't you tell us that evening?"

Otani gave a slight shrug, cradling his bottle and moving on, his wooden *geta* sandals clopping on the unmade road surface. "I don't like to talk about police business at home," he said. "Besides, you all had much more important things to think about. I'm glad Hanae talked you into coming to stay. You probably wouldn't have come to any great harm in the flat but it would have frightened Kazuo-chan. Off tomorrow, then, are you?"

Shimizu smiled with sardonic amusement on hearing the unmistakable note of relief in Otani's voice. "Yes, we'll be leaving you in peace. I sometimes think I was less of a nuisance to you in the old days than I am now." It was Otani's turn to stop and look the other man up and down. It was indeed difficult to see in this composed, intelligent and good-humoured person the ranting, single-minded revolutionary who had screamed slogans and abuse at him and his men during the student riots ten years before.

Otani could smell the tear-gas in his imagination and hear the ritual chanting. "I certainly couldn't imagine what Akiko saw in you," he admitted. "Still, you were a good deal more than a mere nuisance." They walked on and uphill, and rounded the corner leading to the last street of houses before the built-up area gave up the struggle against the shaggy, rocky slopes of Mount Rokko. The Otani house was the last of all, and the soft glow of light through the *shoji* paper of the upper windows was just visible above the high fence.

"Did I tell you we had some excitement over a wild boar that was spotted near here a month or so ago?" Otani asked inconsequentially as they neared the house. Shimizu shook his head. "You have a much more eventful life than I do, nowadays at least."

They went in through the gate and up to the front door. There they both opened their mouths to call out the traditional "I'm back!" but Shimizu beat Otani to it.

It was Hanae's voice which answered "Welcome home!" from the recesses of the kitchen, but Akiko who appeared in the small entrance hall as Otani slipped out of his *geta* and Shimizu bent to take off his shoes. There had been a time when she would have scorned even the slightest recognition of the old ways. Even now her welcoming bow was sketchy and awkward, and her blue jeans and sweater hardly went with the golden gleam of the old tatami mat and the simple flower arrangement in the little alcove behind her. Nevertheless, there was warmth in her manner as she greeted the two men, and Otani reflected that she was a good-looking young woman, in spite of having such a handful as Kazuo to cope with.

"Your father was just saying how much he's looking forward to tomorrow," Shimizu remarked as he stepped up into the hall. "He'll be able to concentrate on his murder properly then."

"Your husband may *look* every inch the rising young business executive," retorted Otani. "Inside he's just as disrespectful as ever to his elders and betters. Who said anything about a murder anyway? Are you suggesting that I'm planning to commit one?"

They moved into the all-purpose downstairs room where the baby was sitting up in the pink plastic prison of a high chair, chewing on the edge of a bib with a cartoon picture of the television character Atom Boy on it; and Otani greeted him gravely.

"What on earth are you two talking about?" Akiko asked with a puzzled smile.

Otani turned to Shimizu in mock exasperation. "I told you I don't like to talk about police business at home," he said. "Now you can see what happens when I do. All I told you was that a foreign businessman died in the earthquake on Saturday. A lot of other people did too. But the foreigner's death involves particular work for us. *Administrative* work," he stressed, glaring at his son-in-law.

Akira Shimizu grinned, quite unabashed. He had something of Kimura in his make-up, Otani thought to himself. "I'm going to have my bath," he said. "We'll get back to your foreigner afterwards. Why, I might even know him." He disappeared with Akiko, and Otani addressed himself to the problem of entertaining his grandson until somebody came to rescue him.

It was not until a good deal later that Shimizu raised the subject again. By then they had finished their evening meal, not without a number of minor crises involving the baby, who was at last asleep on the floor in the corner. The four adults were into the second bottle of *sake*, and Otani was mellow enough to be unbothered by the disorder of the normally clean and tidy room.

"He *was* murdered, wasn't he?" Shimizu asked suddenly, stretching his arms and yawning. All four of them were now wearing cotton *yukatas*, and sat round the low lacquer table set over the *kotatsu* pit in the middle of the room. At this time of year there was no need for any heating, and only Otani dangled his bare feet in the pit from force of habit. The others were perched on their brocaded cushions, Shimizu cross-legged, the women with their legs tucked to one side.

Hanae had been looking rather tired, but now sat up and widened her eyes with interest. "Who?" she enquired, unconsciously holding out her *sake* cup for Akiko to refill. As the junior woman present, Akiko equally mechanically fell into her allotted role and offered the flask all round, after which her husband took it and refilled her own cup for her.

Otani cocked an eyebrow at Shimizu. "What makes you think so?" he demanded.

Shimizu shrugged. "Something about the way you mentioned the death."

He turned to Hanae. "A foreigner was killed the day before yesterday. I heard about it on the way back from the station." Shimizu had never in the years they had known him brought himself to address either Hanae or Otani in any of the accepted forms. The nearest he came to it was in referring to them in conversation with Akiko as "your father" and "your mother". It led to some odd circumlocutions when in their presence.

Otani heaved a sigh. "All right, I'll tell you about it. There isn't a great deal. But please, no gossip outside the family." He smiled over at the baby. "That goes for him too," he said. The level of the *sake* in the bottle went down as Akiko refilled the two small flasks, one in circulation and the other warming in the pan of hot water on a small portable electric ring at her side; but there was no interruption as Otani retailed the account of his drive round Kobe on the afternoon of the earthquake, his discovery of the body and the findings of the medical examiner.

"So," he eventually wound up, "it's an interesting case, but one which I have every intention of leaving to the officer in charge. I am occasionally rude about Inspector Kimura, but he's a clever man, and he understands foreigners. He has a way with the ladies, too. Doesn't he, Ha-chan?"

Hanae sniffed. "It's no use trying to tease me," she said. "I think Kimura-san is very nice, and his private life is no concern of mine."

Shimizu put his *sake* cup down with some care. The drink had loosened all their tongues, and there was a trace of owlish solemnity in his manner as he cut into what looked like turning into rather childish banter. "I don't think you can leave it all to Kimura," he said earnestly, and shook his head from side to side. "I'll tell you why. Because I know a bit about Liebermann-san, that's why."

It took a second or two for Otani to register what he was saying; then the fog cleared and he suddenly felt coolly sober. He sat up straight. "Tell me about him," he said.

Chapter 10

THE COMMITTEE OF THE ROTARY CLUB OF KOBE SOUTH had agonised for some time over the application for membership some years previously on behalf of Tetsuo Otani. Although its membership was not quite so distinguished as that of the older Kobe Central Club it nevertheless included a good many elderly men of wealth and local eminence, of a generation whose opinions of policemen had been formed in the thirties and during the Second World War. In Otani's favour was that he was by any reckoning a senior public servant whose presence would do something to offset the perennially disproportionate number of businessmen. Then again, the club was keen on aiming its philanthropic efforts in such directions as road safety campaigns and the problems of juvenile delinquency, on both of which subjects he might be presumed to speak with authority. Otani was, moreover, the son of the famous Professor Otani whom some of them had known personally. All this neutralised to some extent the distaste many of the members felt at the thought of welcoming a policeman to their company; a representative of the authorities which had banned their beloved organisation during the militaristic years.

As he himself strongly suspected, what had finally tipped

88

the scale in Otani's favour was that he was proposed by no less a person than former Baron Bunsho Maeda. It would have been an intolerable affront to Maeda for his protégé to be blackballed, and Otani had been duly admitted, disarming even a few of the remaining grumblers by the modest courtesy of his speech of thanks on being introduced at the first regular weekly lunchtime meeting after his election. The other Rotarians now all took him completely for granted: most of them gave him a friendly nod as they assembled in the lobby of the New Port Hotel for the twelve-thirty start; and he had even acquired a few cronies.

On the Tuesday following the earthquake there was no other topic of conversation as members swapped experiences and enquired after each other's well-being. The Baron was descended from a family of feudal lords on the island of Shikoku, and Otani found himself thinking of that when he saw his tall, spare figure at one end of the lobby, in a posture of aloof inattentiveness which contrasted sharply with the eager gestures of his companion, a dealer in securities whom Otani had reason to suspect of having been involved in a case of arson in the past.

He hastened over to pay his respects and the Baron detached himself from the one-sided conversation with evident relief. He and Otani offered each other the properly courteous remarks about the weather before passing on to the matter of the earthquake, and had just exchanged the opinion that things could have been worse when the bell rang. As they filed into the private luncheon room the Baron gently insisted that Otani should take a seat at his side. "I want a private word with you, if you have a moment to spare afterwards," he murmured. Since this was almost exactly what Otani had intended to say to Maeda, he was content to do as he was bidden.

Lunch was chicken à la king, which featured on the Rotarians' menu with depressing frequency, and Otani pushed his portion about on the plate without much interest as the next hour passed in desultory conversation and the usual announcements, exhortations, and the introduction of members visiting from other clubs. There was one from Honolulu

West, a noisy fellow who told what Otani supposed must be a funny story in English, and upset the closely calculated timetable.

The consequent reduction in time available for the weekly talk was quite welcome, since it was of more than usual tedium and consisted of a rambling account by an elderly member of a visit he had recently made to Europe. Otani had never in his life been outside Japan and quite failed to understand why so many of his fellow-countrymen seemed unable to stop getting into aeroplanes. Eventually the old gentleman was brought to a halt in mid-sentence when the master of ceremonies rang a bell, and Otani joined in the vigorous general applause. Then the President of the club called for a special contribution from all members, the money to be applied to the relief of people injured in the earthquake, and Otani dug into his wallet with less of a sinking feeling than usual. Rotary really was ruinously expensive; all very well for most of the members for whom a ten-thousand yen note was small change and came off their taxes anyway, but another matter for a public official on a fixed salary. Hardly a week went by without a whip-round for some good cause or another: new flags for the Scouts, an ambulance car for a rural health clinic, or prizes for the winning entries in the primary schoolchildren's painting competition. The usual thousand yen would not do on this occasion, though, and Otani put ten thousand in the plate like most of the others. He would have to explain to Hanae, who took care of their budget in a surprisingly relaxed way, unlike most Japanese wives.

The meeting over punctually at half-past one, Otani followed Maeda out into the lobby. The Baron led the way to an overstuffed sofa in the far corner, still talking amiable trivialities as they went. He settled himself carefully, slender and upright in his expensive London-made suit, fell silent and looked at Otani with his lively eyes. When he spoke again it was with the straightforwardness of many years' acquaintance and with the air of relaxed authority which had always marked his dealings with the younger man. "They tell me that a *gaijin* by the name of Liebermann is dead," he said.

"You knew him." Otani had intended to frame his reply

as a question, but it seemed to come out as a statement, and a vaguely accusatory one which seemed to startle the Baron momentarily. He nodded.

"I'm this year's Chairman of the Chamber of Commerce," he then said easily. "Previously we never admitted foreign members, but in the past two or three years we have. No more than a dozen or so at the moment. The obvious ones: Hong Kong and Shanghai Bank, ICI, Swire"—Maeda rattled off a few more foreign names and initials which meant nothing to Otani—"and although Hochmuth-Wasserman isn't very big, the firm is well regarded. We were quite pleased to have Liebermann. Most of the other foreigners are British or French."

"Well," said Otani carefully, "I can certainly confirm that he's dead. I found him." Maeda's expression did not change, but one silver eyebrow popped up interrogatively, and Otani briefly explained the circumstances. He said nothing of his initial suspicions or of their confirmation by the post-mortem report, and waited for the Baron to react.

"News travels quickly round the business community," he said after a while, "but I certainly hadn't heard that. It explains what I was going to ask you about."

"What was that?" Otani asked in a neutral way.

"Police interest," said Maeda off-handedly. "I was a little puzzled at first. I imagined that your people would have plenty to do after the earthquake without singling out one particular victim for special attention."

It was Otani's turn to be puzzled. "How did you come to hear that we *are* involved?" he enquired.

Maeda waved a hand airily. "My dear Otani-san, I said that news travels quickly. I'm told your men have been frightening the wits out of poor Liebermann's staff since the weekend." It was not perhaps surprising, Otani reflected. A pity in a way that the discovery hadn't been made on May Day or on Constitution Day on the third. That would have given them the rest of Golden Week to look about quietly without generating all this gossip which Maeda seemed to have picked up. He waited, and after a while Maeda went on.

"Then I told myself that you'd naturally have more complicated administrative procedures in the case of a foreigner. I thought I would take the opportunity of seeing you today to confirm my supposition; but of course I now see I was quite wrong. How extraordinary that you of all people should have come upon the poor fellow."

Otani smiled briefly. "Yes, I suppose it was," he said, "but somebody would have done sooner or later, and you're right that when a foreigner dies there are a great many forms to fill in. Especially when there's a doubt about the cause of death."

"*Is* there?" The extreme surprise in the Baron's voice irritated Otani, who responded more bluntly than he would normally have dreamed of doing to his old commander.

"Why shouldn't we be doubtful?" he demanded. "It isn't as if the ceiling fell on him."

Maeda nodded. "Of course, of course," he said reasonably. "What you probably don't know, though, is that he had a very bad heart. I've seen him myself in distress at meetings. He had some pills he used to take. I read of several cases of death through shock on Boys' Day: I must say I felt distinctly shaky myself at the time. I just automatically assumed that it proved too much for Liebermann. He was getting on, you know."

"Fifty-eight," said Otani, still curtly.

The Baron looked at Otani quizzically. "You seem to be not quite your usual self," he said. "Ah . . . is something troubling you?"

Otani sat back, avoiding Maeda's eye. "It's a bit difficult," he said. "As a matter of fact, I'm glad to hear you knew him. In the Chamber of Commerce context. I supposed you would at least know of this *gaijin*'s existence, and I was hoping to see you here today to ask you about him. I'm finding it hard to form an idea of the man. My son-in-law tells me he had a certain reputation in Japanese business circles."

The Baron's aristocratic features revealed little, but his voice sounded wary. "What did your son-in-law say? Doesn't he work for my competitors in Osaka?" Maeda knew quite well where Shimizu worked, and Otani knew that he knew, so he ignored the second question and pondered briefly before replying to the first.

"I was quite surprised," he said then. "I mentioned Liebermann's name casually, and he told me that he had met the man himself. That he spoke astonishingly good Japanese for a man who had been here for only a few years; that he entertained lavishly, especially young executives like my son-in-law, and that he seemed very inquisitive about businesses unconnected with his own." Otani paused. "Also that his wife is having an affair with a Japanese actor in Osaka," he added.

As if on cue, Maeda fixed his gaze on a large model of Osaka Castle which stood in a glass case in the middle of the lobby. Two blue-rinsed women, obviously American, were discussing it earnestly. Apart from themselves, all the Rotarians had departed. "Interesting," he said after a while. "I'm not surprised that Liebermann paid some attention to young Shimizu. He had a nose for the young men who will get to the top in business. All the same I think your son-in-law is letting his imagination run away with him."

He looked at Otani intently, and his manner became persuasive. "I really don't think there was anything particularly odd about Liebermann's behaviour, you know," he said. "We all keep our eyes and ears open about what's going on in the big corporations. That's how business opportunities are picked up."

Otani was not to be so easily headed off. "Fluent Japanese? Lavish entertaining? His office didn't strike me as being specially impressive. And the thing about the wife? They all seem rather unexpected." The manner in which he fired off the questions was still far from deferential.

The Baron for his part was clearly choosing his words with some care, but replied calmly and judiciously. "Certainly Liebermann spoke good Japanese," he agreed. "A number of my foreign acquaintances do. I wouldn't agree that it was in any way astonishing, though. Why, he might easily have picked it up in the war—he was old enough. I had you taught Russian," he said accusingly to Otani. "Waste of time. You were hopeless." He smiled reminiscently, and Otani grinned. It was the first break in the tension.

"As to the entertaining, again I think Shimizu overstates it. One may entertain modestly and often or lavishly and seldom. The second method sticks in people's minds more, and creates a reputation." He stopped for a moment, and what looked to Otani like a spasm of pain passed over his lean face. "The wife? Yes. I *have* heard gossip about her. Not an actor, you know. A *bunraku* puppeteer. I'm an honorary member of the board of the *bunraku* company and I . . . ah . . . know the man in question." Otani noticed that Maeda was beginning to fumble for words. "Understandable, you know, Otani-san. Irmgard Liebermann is a great deal younger than her . . . husband, and a very interesting, intelligent woman."

Otani raised an eyebrow. "You know her well?"

Maeda nodded. "I first met her at a reception for a German trade mission about a year ago and she sought me out and told me that she had heard of my interest in *bunraku*. I was amazed at how much she knew about the finer points of puppetry. Then later on I heard of her . . . friendship . . . with Dangoro." He paused awkwardly, and Otani made a mental note of what was obviously a stage name. Maeda leaned forward to Otani. "Tell me, how is she taking all this?"

"I don't know," Otani confessed. "We can't seem to find her." The Baron uncrossed his legs and crossed them again the other way, and Otani debated with himself whether to try to force him to define more precisely his relationship with the Liebermanns. Certainly first Akira Shimizu and now Maeda seemed to know a great deal more about them than either he or Kimura did, and Shimizu had implied that Maeda might have business dealings of some sort with the German.

The possibility that Liebermann might be the owner of the gun taken by the boy Oda was a very long shot indeed and Otani took Kimura's word for it that Liebermann had a clean record as far as the authorities were concerned. Any irregularity in his wife's love-life would have been of no interest to the police, and though Kimura enjoyed gossip he was neither required nor disposed to spy on foreign residents unless they forced themselves on his attention. Otani wondered whether to tell Maeda openly that Liebermann had been killed and observe his reaction, but was spared the necessity to make up his mind.

The Baron rose to his feet and Otani hastened to follow suit. "I'm sorry. I have taken up too much of your time."

The tall slender old man straightened the beautiful knot of his silk tie and shook his head. He looked sad to Otani's eyes. "No, no," he said, "I am a lazy old man who leaves the work to others nowadays. I really don't think that I can help you, though . . . except that I'll see if I can get in touch with Irmgard-san for you. All this is . . . very distressing. Poor woman. I do hope that any doubts you have will soon be put at rest."

He set off towards the automatic doors, and Otani followed. The doors were propped wide open to the warm sunshine while apparently undergoing repairs. The two men stood outside for a moment before separating. "Liebermann was a very sick man, you know," said the Baron, looking intently into Otani's eyes. "Ah, here comes my car." A large black Nissan limousine drew up and the driver jumped out to open the door for him. "May I offer you a ride?" Otani declined politely and bowed as Maeda settled himself in the back. "I will do my best to find her for you, Otani-san," he said, "but please don't harry the poor woman if you can help it." He nodded, and the driver closed the door on him.

Otani gave a cheery little wave as the car swept the old man away, then turned thoughtfully to walk back to his office.

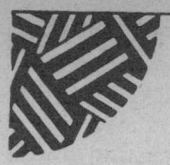

Chapter 11

IT WAS OBVIOUSLY NECESSARY TO OPEN THE SEALED EN-velope containing the articles taken by Otani from Lieber-mann's body; and Kimura was irritated when he went up to the first floor on arrival, after pausing to let the elderly duty constable at the main entrance laboriously log him in, only to learn from Migishima that the Old Man was out. Rotary day too, so he probably wouldn't be back before two at the earliest.

He consoled himself rapidly. The aftermath of the earth-quake entailed a huge amount of purely administrative work for the police, and Otani would be kept quite busy enough scrutinising and adding his personal seal to all the reports flowing in from the divisional offices, traffic police and other departments.

The three most senior non-uniformed officers under Ota-ni's command were himself, Ninja Noguchi and old ramrod Sakamoto. Fate had given him this case, and as a conse-quence Sakamoto was upset. Too bad. A foreigner was a for-eigner, and foreigners were Kimura's business; except for the Koreans and the Chinese, of course. Noguchi took care of them, and quite right too. More than something of a snob, Kimura much preferred hobnobbing with well-to-do busi-

96

ness and consular residents, and in their case even overcame his distaste for Africans and Indians. The Liebermann murder was *his* case, and there was no need to go running to Otani every five minutes.

He had quite recovered his normal good humour by the time he made his way along the ground-floor corridor towards his sanctum. Most of the reeded glass partitions on either side of the corridor had been shattered on Boys' Day, and the glaziers of Kobe had so much business on hand that it would be some time before anyone would get round to fixing them. Kimura glanced with mild curiosity into rooms he had never had occasion to enter, nodding affably to those colleagues who were at their desks. Proceeding on his amiable way, he was brought up short by a glare of gloomy ferocity from Inspector Sakamoto, who was sitting bolt upright at his tiny desk confronting the single sheet of paper on its surface. A ruler, pencil and telephone were lined up with geometrical precision as though for questioning, and the rest of the room was equally bare and disciplined.

As head of the criminal investigation section, Sakamoto was theoretically the chief of Otani's detectives. He disapproved of Kimura and his ways with a thoroughgoing bitterness which quite distressed Kimura, who enjoyed the pretended exasperations of Otani and usually knew just how far he could push the Superintendent before things became serious. Sakamoto was another matter, and Kimura sometimes found himself wondering what he had been during the war. A grizzled, skinny little man in his fifties, he could have been a militarist of the deepest dye with the blood of hundreds on his hands; but as a bit of an amateur psychologist Kimura thought it more likely that he had been a drill corporal on a parade ground or even a dish washer in a cookhouse and was now overcompensating.

"Good morning, Sakamoto-san," he said, politely coming to a halt in the corridor and putting his head through the empty windowframe. "I expect you're very busy." The greeting was unexceptionally conventional, but Kimura could not resist accompanying it with a glance at the naked desk and single sheet of paper. The resulting irony was not lost on

Sakamoto, who had the not unusual capacity to take offence at even quite innocent remarks.

"My door is closed," he barked, switching his gaze back to the desk.

"True," Kimura conceded, withdrawing his head. He prepared to go on his way, then had second thoughts.

Stepping back a pace, he rapped on the door. "Come in!" The response was immediate, and Kimura shook his head as he opened the door. Stark, raving mad.

"I am intruding," he said formally as he stepped into the egg-box of a room.

Sakamoto looked up, focusing his stare in the region of Kimura's throat. "What is it?" he demanded peremptorily. His face was as wrinkled and looked as sour as a pickled plum.

"I should be much obliged for your advice in a matter concerning the case I am investigating with the expert assistance of two of your officers—for which I am most grateful," Kimura said.

Sakamoto took a deep breath as though about to explode in outrage, then thought better of it. The line of demarcation of their respective spheres of responsibility was clear enough most of the time. Foreigners seldom committed criminal offences in Hyogo Prefecture though they were forever running foul of administrative regulations, particularly by forgetting to renew their visas. Moreover, criminals were rarely mixed up with foreigners of the kind it pleased Kimura to interest himself in. It was for Superintendent Otani to allot responsibility and deploy resources in cases of doubt, and he had unambiguously and in writing informed Sakamoto that Kimura was in charge of looking into the death of the German businessman.

Instead of speaking, Sakamoto therefore pointed silently to the hard wooden chair facing the desk and raised a vestigial eyebrow. The few seconds' delay while Kimura adjusted the crease of his trousers to his satisfaction after sitting down gave them both time to decide on their tactics. They both spoke at once, using the same phrase, as though at a signal, "As a matter of fact . . ." then broke off and extended a palm to each other in invitation to proceed. Kimura thought it only fair to let Sakamoto win the little bout of courtesy which ensued, and cleared his throat.

"I realise that you have had the heavy responsibility of headquarters duty officer since the day of the earthquake in addition to your normal burden," he said in a conciliatory way, "and I hesitate to trouble you. As I know you are aware, the Superintendent personally discovered the body of a foreign resident, a businessman, on the evening of Boys' Day. He placed the articles he took from the man's body in an envelope and sealed it."

Sakamoto continued to stare at Kimura's neck. "Very proper," he said sternly.

Kimura pressed on. "Normally the envelope would be handed intact to the man's legal personal representative. It has been discovered, however, that the man did not die from natural causes. There are therefore two points upon which I should be grateful for your views. First, do you agree with me that the contents of the envelope are to be regarded as evidence?" Sakamoto pretended to give weighty consideration to the issue, but the answer was so obvious that he had no alternative but to nod assent.

"Thank you," said Kimura sweetly. Not all the courses of action which struck him as perfectly reasonable appeared later in that light to Otani, and the endorsement of Sakamoto the arch-proceduralist would constitute a complete answer to any reproach which might be levelled at him in this instance. "Well then, Sakamoto-san. May I trespass on your patience by asking you to witness my breaking of the Superintendent's seal and to agree an inventory of the articles in the envelope?"

Sakamoto was not happy, and pursed his thin lips. "Why do you not ask the Superintendent? It is his seal you are proposing to break."

Kimura delved into his pocket, producing a packet of Peace cigarettes and pulled one out with his lips in a laconic gesture which it had needed a great deal of practice in front of the mirror to perfect. He lit it and sat in the middle of a dense cloud of smoke looking at Sakamoto through narrowed Bogartian eyes.

"I should not dream of troubling the Superintendent with such a trivial matter," he said at last. "He has more important things to do than sit beside me looking at every piece of potential evidence in a case he has instructed me to investigate."

Sakamoto cocked his head on one side like an elderly and offended parrot. "But Inspector Sakamoto does *not* have anything more important to do, in Inspector Kimura's distinguished opinion," he said huffily, making his own rank sound dignified and Kimura's like a bogus degree.

Kimura shrugged and got up. "I am sorry to have troubled you," he said curtly. "It occurred to me that you might be willing to give me the benefit of your long experience. I will therefore consult Noguchi-san instead." This did the trick. If there was one officer in the whole Prefectural force whom Sakamoto disliked more than Kimura himself it was Ninja Noguchi. Kimura's lackadaisical foppishness was bad enough, but Noguchi's sloppy, beery, unwashed approach to his duties revolted Sakamoto's very soul.

"Wait," he said, waving Kimura down again into the chair. "I fail to see that your case is of any concern to the Drugs Section. On the other hand it is clearly a criminal matter. It is all most unfortunate. Had it not happened on a public holiday it would no doubt have been handled through the *proper* channels from the first." He glared at Kimura as he emphasised the word. "One hesitates to question the Superintendent's judgment in placing you in charge and giving you half my staff into the bargain." He seemed to realise as he spoke that he was at last making Kimura really angry, and hastily back-tracked. "Though of course you have a clear interest in the matter," he conceded manfully. "Let us by all means open the envelope together."

Kimura's good humour returned as the older man tailed off lamely, and he stood up again cheerfully. "I'll go and get it," he said. Sakamoto half closed his eyes in mental anguish as he heard Kimura whistling on his way down the corridor, while he clattered the door of his locker open then slammed it shut, and on the way back. It often seemed to Sakamoto that he was the only person in the building with a sense of discipline.

Kimura was back in less than a minute with the bulky manila envelope which he dumped on Sakamoto's desk. "Got an inventory form?" he demanded briskly.

Sakamoto looked at him with wintry rectitude. "Of course," he said, and opened one of the drawers of his desk. Within, meticulously arranged, were supplies of every conceivable official form. Sakamoto selected the appropriate one, carefully rearranged the others, and closed the drawer. He then put the single sheet which had been on his desk into another drawer and lined up the form foursquare in front of himself in its place. Kimura watched, fascinated. His own administrative methods were surprisingly tidy, but this man was in a different league.

Sakamoto next reached into yet another drawer and produced a pair of scissors which he laid on the desk in front of Kimura, careful to avoid the discourtesy of actually handing a sharp instrument to another person. "*Dozo*. Go ahead," he said. Kimura pulled his chair round to the side of the desk, took up the envelope and scissors and cut the flap. He then carefully withdrew the contents and peered inside to make sure that it was empty before handing it to Sakamoto to do the same.

Chapter 12

Two hours later Kimura sat in his own little office contemplating a sheet of paper headed with the printed words

HYOGO PREFECTURAL POLICE
Inventory of Articles retained for Inspection

The remainder of the sheet was completed in Sakamoto's neat and fussy handwriting. He still used the old-fashioned steel nib, and Kimura had to admit that the result gave a better impression than his own efforts with ballpoint or felt-tip. Kimura lined up the articles in a semicircle round his blotter as he went through the list again.

> Description and itemised list of articles removed from the body of LIEBERMANN Richard and placed under seal by OTANI Tetsuo, Superintendent, Hyogo Prefectural Police. Seal broken by KIMURA Jiro in the presence of SAKAMOTO Masao, both Inspectors assigned to the said force.
> 1 Leather billfold, brown, containing Yen 27,500 in notes
> 2 Yen 480 in coin

3 Metal ring with two car keys, serial numbers
   F638 and B244
4 Air letter from D. Schultz, Stuttgart, Germany, addressed to Liebermann at business
   office
5 Letter from Nakajima Tadao, Yokohama,
   addressed as above
6 Airmail letter from D. Schultz addressed as
   above
7 Leather wallet, black, containing: Alien's
   registration card for subject
   9 business cards for subject
   Receipted bill from Okura Hotel, Tokyo
   American Express credit card
   Photograph of man, presumed subject, with
   dog
   Four pharmaceutical pills enclosed in separate foil wrappers
   One ticket for matinée performance *bunraku*
   puppet theatre, Osaka, 8 May

He really had to make up his mind about the theatre. It was already after one, and the performance was due to begin at four. A single ticket might mean nothing. The person in the next seat could be a perfect stranger to Liebermann, and almost certainly would be to Kimura. Maybe Liebermann just happened to be fond of the *bunraku*.

Kimura turned to the sheets clipped to the back of the inventory. They contained translations of the two letters from D. Schultz of Stuttgart, made for him by his own staff. The Foreign Residents Supervision Section consisted of less than half a dozen plainclothes officers, but between them Kimura and his men could manage the major European languages, plus Russian, Cantonese and of course Korean. The letter from Yokohama was in English anyway, and seemed to concern a straightforward business transaction.

He scanned again the letters from the affectionate Dagmar Schultz. She seemed to be on intimate terms with Liebermann, whom she addressed as ''Sweetest Rikki''. Not that the actual texts were particularly steamy. The air letter was quite old, dated in February; the second, 23 April. Liebermann must have received it just before Golden Week. The two of them had evidently met somewhere, since in the first letter Dagmar talked about seeing him soon and in the second thanked him for a wonderful time. At the Okura in Tokyo perhaps? It could have been anywhere; in Germany even. They would have to check whether Liebermann had left the country recently.

The rendezvous must have been satisfactory. The first letter ended "I love you", and the second "I adore you". So. Here was a reasonably well-off businessman, getting on in years, receiving letters at his office from a lady friend in Germany. Not so very unusual or terrible. It was the postscript that decided Kimura to go to Osaka, even though his German translator had not been quite sure that he had deciphered the scrawl accurately. He had finally plumped for the view that it said "I hope Dangoro is keeping her happy still—the man with the magic fingers! But not like my Rikki!"

Kimura's cultural interests were far from highbrow. He much preferred the cinema to the live theatre, except for occasional visits to the all-girl revues at Takarazuka. He found these pleasurably sexy, especially the lesbian overtones of the glamorous duets and tangos with the male roles taken by svelte women in elegantly cut jackets and trousers. He had only rarely seen *kabuki*, and had never set foot in a *noh* or *bunraku* theatre. Nevertheless, he had a vague notion that Dangoro was a *bunraku* stage name, and one of his more cultivated assistants confirmed it; adding the information that the incumbent Dangoro was the thirteenth of the line, his teacher Dangoro XII having conferred the illustrious name on him two or three years earlier.

It was a lead of a kind, and Kimura always enjoyed getting out of the office. He fiddled with the button on his smart electronic watch and squinted at the display. Nearly half past one. It might just be wise to be on his way before Otani came back. After a moment's final hesitation he slipped the theatre ticket into his pocket before locking the rest of Liebermann's relics in his steel cupboard and sauntering out of the building. Time for a quick snack before catching the Hanshin line express to Osaka. Even so, he was in Osaka within an hour and looking about him interestedly in the lobby of the Asahi-za Theatre at Dotombori soon after three-thirty. Kimura quite liked going to any sort of public event in Osaka. It was not that the people seemed any more prosperous or well-dressed than those of Kobe, but there was an undeniable big-city alertness about them which he was always at a loss to account for. Most of the older Japanese women gossiping among themselves were wearing light summery kimonos, but Kimura did not see a single man dressed in the old style as he stood dealing with a second snack, of rice balls wrapped in seaweed wafers.

There was a surprising number of Westerners among the people assembling and now gradually making their way into the auditorium. Kimura did not at once recognise Ilse Fischer. The blond hair which had been pulled back severely when he met her in her office now fell about her face and made her look younger and softer, and she was wearing a delicate lavender dress which set off her colouring admirably. The neckline, though entirely seemly, revealed the creamy uplands of what must definitely be very handsome breasts.

Kimura moved unobtrusively behind a group of noisily chattering people and stood quietly thinking. Would she turn out to be his neighbour in the next seat? Hardly. If she had planned to accompany her employer to the theatre it would be extraordinarily coldblooded on her part to go all the same, knowing that he was lying dead in the city mortuary.

No, there must be some other reason for her presence there. The May sunshine was very warm, even hot, and he was glad that he had decided to put on his new "energy saving" cotton safari suit that morning. He reflected that he must look very different from the inquisitorial official in the business suit of two days before, and felt reasonably confident that she would not recognise him. A glutinous female voice made itself heard over the public address system, offering effusive thanks to the patrons of the performance and warning them that it was about to begin, and Miss Fischer made her way into the auditorium without a backward glance. Kimura was able to slip in well behind her and watch her take a seat near the front, over to the left. An attendant scrutinised the ticket he had extracted from Liebermann's belongings, and he was relieved to find himself seated in the centre block, a good deal further back. The seat to his left was occupied by an old man in a business suit who seemed to be studying a copy of the script; while after a few moments the one on his right was taken by one of two middle-aged women who were evidently together. Total strangers: so far, so good.

The first play was *Kanjincho*, and Kimura became even more confused when, after the always startling dramatic warning clatter of the Chinese blocks, the curtain swept aside to reveal not conventional scenery but a typical *noh* stage background showing a stylised pine tree painted on a wooden wall. This, the programme advised him, was intended to represent the military checkpoint at Ataka through which the fugitive hero Yoshitsune, his doughty retainer Benkei and their companions were to attempt to pass.

Kimura nearly disgraced himself by giggling when the principal puppets appeared, each manipulated by no fewer than three men, while the *joruri* reciter began the narration in a strangulated voice, kneeling in formal kimono before a low lectern at one side of the stage with the *shamisen* players plucking the strings of their banjo-like instruments beside him. The stage looked impossibly crowded with the chief manipulators in plain view in their dark kimonos holding the puppets from the back with the left hand and directing the dolls' right arms with the other. Each had two black-gowned and hooded assistants, one to manipulate the left arm of the puppet and the other its legs. There was such a crowd on stage that at first it looked more like a rehearsal to Kimura than an actual performance.

After a few minutes, though, an odd magic began to work, and the human figures seemed to fade and become insubstantial before Kimura's eyes as the puppets sucked the life from them and gradually came to dominate the stage and his consciousness. They were in any case beautiful things; about two-thirds life-sized and robed in the most gorgeous brocades. As the reciter chanted the dialogue, assuming different voices for each character, his face red and contorted with strain, so the eyes of the dolls moved, their eyebrows rose in surprise, the mouths opened and closed and the hands and arms gestured with the most convincingly natural grace imaginable.

Before long Kimura's disbelief was entirely suspended, and he became absorbed in the drama being played out before him. The *shamisen* accompaniment *was* the wind and the rain, and the choking gurgles and moans of the reciter seemed almost by a feat of ventriloquism to emerge from the painted wooden mouths of the puppets.

By the time the play was over Kimura had nearly forgotten why he was in the theatre at all, and during the applause had to rouse himself from something of a daze as people all round gathered their belongings and made for the exits and refreshments, looking across the half-empty auditorium just in time to see Ilse Fischer stand up and start moving not towards one of the ordinary exits but to what looked like a pass-door giving access to the backstage area.

Without stopping to think, he hurried down the aisle and caught up with her just as she was opening the door. "Well, hello, Miss Fischer!" he said chirpily. She turned and looked at him with a startled expression, then the colour drained from her face as he added, "Jiro Kimura, Hyogo Police. Remember me?" For a moment Kimura thought she was going to faint, then with what was clearly a supreme effort she brought herself under control, and Kimura watched with fascination as she thought herself frantically into an appropriate reaction to his appearance before her.

"Oh, Mr Kimura. I am sorry . . . I was just so startled to see you here." He crinkled a warm smile at her, and gestured to an empty seat in the front row. "Won't you sit down a moment?" he suggested. "You look kind of bushed." This was a new idiom he was using for the first time, and he was not quite sure that he had the context right, but Miss Fischer nodded anyway, closed the pass-door again and then sat down with deliberation. "Never would I think you are interested in the *bunraku*," she said carefully. Kimura decided to add to the confusion of thoughts that were obviously racing through her mind.

"I'm not," he said blandly. "I never set foot in this place before in my life. Heard of it of course. In fact I remember when it was called the Bunraku-za; I never could figure out why they changed the name. I'm surprised it's so modern inside. I thought the *bunraku* puppets were more or less a thing of the past."

He nodded towards the pass-door. "I'm sorry, am I keeping you?" Miss Fischer swallowed, then seemed to come to a decision. "As a matter of fact, I was going to meet a . . . friend of Frau Liebermann in the company. I was thinking he might know where she is . . . unless perhaps you have already heard from her?"

"Not yet," Kimura said. "Frankly, we shall have to go all out to find her if she doesn't show up soon." He felt he needed time to think himself. "May I join you?" He made to get up, but she put out a hand quickly to restrain him.

"Please, no. Not now. He has in the second play a very big part. Perhaps—perhaps after the performance." It was true that a few of the audience were already beginning to drift back, some of them carrying snack boxes with them, and Kimura noticed a fat woman in an unsuitably colourful kimono glaring at him meaningly as she bore down towards them. He must be in her seat.

Kimura got up and smiled ingratiatingly at the fat woman, then nodded to Miss Fischer. "Okay," he said. "Let's meet right here at the end of the performance." He made his way quickly back to his seat, not bothering to watch from the tail of his eye. If she did not keep the appointment she would have even more awkward questions to answer than if she did.

Nevertheless, Kimura was exasperated when he did after a while look in her direction and saw no sign of her, and almost started to run out of the theatre in pursuit. Then he settled back philosophically into his seat and studied the programme. A big part, she had said, and there he was, listed as principal manipulator of Tokubei, the hero of *Sonezaki Shinju*, lover of Ohatsu the courtesan. It would be perfectly possible to form an initial impression of this Dangoro person

108

when he appeared on stage. All the better even, since he would have no idea that he was being observed from Kimura's professional point of view.

When the curtain was swept aside Kimura was again smitten with a sense of the ridiculous, and once again it was very soon replaced by a mood of childlike wonder. He concentrated as firmly as he could on the face of Dangoro, majestic in the formal *kamishimo* kimono of mediaeval times, and saw the features of a man of about forty, with a lean, conventionally handsome face. After a minute or so, though, it was as if all the puppeteers became translucent again, and Kimura was caught up once more in spite of himself.

By the time the scene changed to the Temmaya teahouse and Ohatsu had hidden her lover Tokubei beneath the voluminous skirts of her kimono while the narrator assumed her voice to speak of death, Kimura felt a distinct pricking behind the eyes, and pulled himself back to reality with an effort. He looked in the direction of the German woman and with some surprise saw what he was almost sure was her blond head. So she was back. Well, whatever she had been doing, it could hardly have involved Dangoro, who had been on stage throughout.

Eventually it was over, and when the lights went up Kimura was able to satisfy himself that Ilse Fischer was indeed back in her seat and intending to wait for him as agreed. As he approached her for the second time she gave a timid smile, seeming to have recovered some of her composure. She nevertheless exhibited virtually text-book indications of furtiveness and Kimura began to think that he might have stumbled on something of significance.

''What did you think, Mr Kimura?'' she asked.

''Marvellous,'' he said simply. ''I had no idea it would be like that.''

Ilse Fischer looked at him as though to satisfy herself about his sincerity. ''Why are you here?'' she blurted out then, and drew her bottom lip between her teeth, apparently quite hard.

Kimura decided on a shot in the dark. ''The same reason as you are, I should think. A suggestion was made that Liebermann might have contacts at the theatre here.'' Her eyes widened satisfactorily, and Kimura went on, suddenly inspired. "I could have had Osaka Police check it out for me, but I thought it might cause less bother if I came and asked around quietly myself."

It was like putting money in a slot machine and winning the jackpot. Ilse Fischer shook her head violently. "No. Not questions, please. I have said already, Frau Liebermann has a . . . good friend in the company. He can perhaps say where she is. I will introduce you him." Her hand was on Kimura's arm, pleadingly, and he felt a lurch of attraction to her as she went on. "Please—I will explain after—please do not say who you are. Please, pretend to be a friend from me and I will ask him about Frau Liebermann." She looked at him nervously and Kimura found himself touched by her incompetence. "Do you understand German?"

"No," he said truthfully, then cursed himself as he saw the relief in her troubled hazel eyes. He made up his mind. "Okay, go ahead . . . Ilse," he said in a voice which set out to be businesslike but was rendered a little uncertain by an unaccountable dryness in his throat.

She looked at him intently, even in her flat-heeled sandals fully as tall as he, hesitated, then made for the pass-door without another word. Kimura followed, and found himself in a different world. The contrast between the auditorium and the backstage area was like travelling in time from the late twentieth century back to the middle ages. The broad corridor was only dimly lit, and seemed to be filled with scurrying, mysterious minions in dusty black cotton gowns, carrying dolls, costumes and props between the storerooms and the wings.

Ilse seemed to know her way about and to be accepted by the stage-hands and assistant puppeteers, one or two of whom nodded in recognition as they passed. She led the way towards a sizable dressing-room, brightly lit, and slipped off her sandals as she stepped up on the tatami matting from the concrete floor of the corridor, beckoning Kimura to follow. Dangoro was with another man inside. Both were kneeling in front of an illuminated mirror, still dressed in their stage costumes. The second man was elderly, with a serenely magnificent face, and they both smiled in welcome as Ilse greeted them and apologised for the intrusion—in excellent Japanese.

Taken aback, Kimura was in any case at a loss for words, as she went on to present him to the two men, listening in mounting amazement as she uttered a number of fluent, grammatical and extravagantly untruthful sentences about him, introducing him as a Japanese-American assistant professor from Oregon making his first extended visit to Japan. "It must seem strange to you, but Matsuda-sensei understands only a little Japanese," she concluded in that language, before turning to Kimura with a bright false smile and adding in her Teutonic English, "Did you understand a little, Bob? I was telling to them that you are like many *nisei* and not knowing even a little bit your ancestral language."

Kimura hastily sank to his knees and bowed to the two puppeteers in response to the grave inclination of their heads in his direction. He had been partially prepared to go along with a modest degree of duplicity, if only because Ilse seemed to be serving into her own net with such consistency, but this was ridiculous. Nevertheless, as he strove to keep up with events he was encouraged by the thought that he must look so idiotically uncomprehending that the two men might just be taken in by the extraordinary charade Ilse had embarked upon.

He jolted his mind back to English and tried to expand himself into the marginally larger-than-Japanese personality he supposed to be appropriate for an American from the West Coast. "Right, Ilse," he said heartily. "I guess I got the general idea, but not a lot more. I'd like you to tell these gentlemen from me that I thought the show was just great. Really great." He beamed, and listened fascinated as she translated what he had said into his own language for the benefit of the two dignified performers in their archaic dress. Whatever game Ilse was up to, it was almost enjoyable for its own sake.

It was more difficult when the older man responded for them both, smiling kindly at Kimura and articulating his words with helpful emphasis as he welcomed the foreign visitor and trusted he would enjoy his stay in Japan. Kimura

111

managed to assume a look of tolerant incomprehension, nodding from time to time and helped a little by the dream-like appearance of the room. A number of *bunraku* puppets were dangling lifelessly from racks along one wall, and at a word from his senior, Dangoro rose smoothly from his knees and took one down.

Kimura recognised it as Tokubei from the last play, and watched with unaffected fascination as the puppeteer removed the head from the simple framework of the body and demonstrated how by pulling and releasing hidden strings the eyes, eyebrows and lips could be moved. The effect was surrealistic and oddly unnerving, especially when the senior puppeteer began to match Dangoro's actions with a fragment of the appropriate dialogue. Kimura was slightly relieved when the doll was returned to the rack, the head once more in place and drooping; a piece of inanimate wood. Dangoro then suggested that they might go to another room, the old man accepted their excuses with incurious good humour, and they left him in peace before his make-up mirror.

Dangoro led the way to a kind of waiting-room in a side corridor. This was furnished with Western-style easy-chairs upholstered in an unsuitable acid green, and the puppeteer settled himself in one with a rustling of the stiff folds of his heavy silken kimono. In normal lighting and the everyday surroundings of the drab little room he looked now to be a thoroughly twentieth-century man in spite of his theatrical clothes. He seemed to be on easy terms with Ilse and had chatted in a straightforward social manner in Japanese while coming along the corridor, asking polite questions about Kimura's impressions of Japan in general and of Osaka and the *bunraku* theatre in particular.

"I'm very sorry I can't offer you much in the way of refreshments," he said when they were all seated. "Perhaps some green tea, though?" He prepared to clap his hands to summon an attendant, but Ilse stopped him, saying something in what was obviously German. A shadow passed over Dangoro's face and he responded rapidly in the same language.

After a further quick-fire exchange Ilse turned to Kimura,

an apologetic half-smile on her face. "I am very sorry, Bob," she said in English, and Kimura noticed that she seemed to have as much trouble with the letter "r" as he did with "l". At least, it sounded strangely but not unpleasantly throaty. "Dangoro and I speak German mostly together. 'Dangoro' is his stage name of course. He was a . . . what is it . . . kind of student assistant and was given this name 'Dangoro' when he first was made principal puppeteer."

Kimura waved his hand in a "go ahead" gesture. "How did Mr Dangoro come to speak German?" he enquired.

Ilse giggled attractively: it was her first spontaneously amiable action. "Not *Mister* Dangoro," she said. "Just Dangoro," apparently congratulating Kimura on his suitably inept mistake. "The Bunraku-za sent a company on Europe tour it was a few years," she said. "In Dusseldorf Dangoro was invited to help the State Theatre as a kind of adviser. Maybe they would start a puppet theatre, but nothing came from it—except that Dangoro can now speak wonderful German."

Dangoro sat quietly through all this, calmly looking Kimura up and down. Kimura began to have an uneasy suspicion that Dangoro was not convinced of his bona fides as an American academic. He could hardly blame him, and would have very much liked to get on to the subject of Irmgard Liebermann, however obliquely. It was difficult to see how he could broach it himself.

Ilse reverted to Japanese, explaining to Dangoro what she had been telling Kimura, and Dangoro gestured self-deprecatingly. He seemed patient enough, but wary. Switching back to German, Ilse went on speaking to Dangoro at some length. Kimura was almost sure that he caught the name "Irmgard" once or twice, but would not have been able to swear to it. He abandoned any hope of interpreting even the basic drift of Ilse's words, except that she spoke in a serious, intent way and seemed to be trying to convince Dangoro of something.

Instead Kimura concentrated on watching their faces. Europeans always revealed much more in their expressions than Japanese, but in his experience Europeans were more adept in deceit. He could hardly ever tell from Otani's face what he was thinking; only from his choice of words. With some Englishmen, on the other hand, a bland poker face was a sure sign of an outright lie. Ilse's expression as she spoke, though strained, made her face look younger and more ardent than in repose, and the wide mouth was generous and forthcoming. She fell silent at last and Dangoro replied, speaking with apparent fluency and in level, quiet tones. He looked serious but not particularly anxious, and seemed to be trying to reassure Ilse and calm her down.

The exchange completed, Ilse turned to Kimura and apologised again. "What will you think from me, Bob!" she said.

"Don't mention it," Kimura reassured her. "It's been a great pleasure visiting with Mr . . . ah, with Dangoro here. I guess perhaps we ought to be going, though?" He made movements preparatory to getting up and observed that Dangoro followed suit with an alacrity that verged on the discourteous.

They all rose, and Kimura stuck out a hand in Dangoro's direction manfully, as naturally as he was able to bring himself to do it. Dangoro shook hands cordially, looking Kimura straight in the eye as he did so. "You greeted us with a very courteous bow in the dressing-room, Matsuda-san," he said rapidly in Japanese. "I am glad to see you know the ways of this country as well as those of America."

"It's the German way too," Ilse chimed in hurriedly, extending her own hand which Dangoro also shook, giving her a curious glance as he did so.

Then the two of them were on their way towards the stage door, but not before Kimura from the corner of his eye noticed a grim set to Dangoro's mouth as they turned away. He waited till they were in the mild evening air of the street before saying anything to Ilse. Then he turned on her, oblivious to the obstruction he thus constituted to passers-by. "You owe me an explanation," he said bleakly in Japanese, dropping completely his normal air of playboy gallantry.

"Very well," Ilse replied, also in Japanese. "Not here in the middle of Dotombori, though. Will you buy me dinner?" Her fluency impressed Kimura, who had been making a men-

114

tal note of the many errors she had made when speaking English, which he would have supposed a good deal easier for her.

He glared at her a little longer, then nodded curtly. "Agreed," he said, "provided that you answer my questions straightforwardly." She said nothing, so he took her elbow, spun her around, and marched her off in the direction of Yodoyabashi.

They walked in silence for a while, Kimura reflecting that his impulse in using the ticket from Liebermann's wallet had probably amounted to a flash of genius. "I could have taken you to the Argo—the French restaurant right across from the theatre," he said out of the blue after a while. "They say it's quite good. I know, what about one of the German restaurants? You can tell me what to order."

Ilse stopped short. "Please," she said in an exasperated voice, "we need to talk quietly, and that does *not* mean being deafened by a lot of drunks banging on the tables in the Rosenkeller."

Kimura shrugged. "Whatever you say," he agreed, walking on. "I'll take you to an Italian place I know not far from the station. It's quiet." He deliberately walked fast so that she had to take a hurried step or two to catch up, and neither spoke again until they were inside the Abela restaurant at Umeda.

"Well, that's something, at least," Otani said grimly as he put the telephone down and looked across at Noguchi. Noguchi's battered features seemed to remain immobile, but an interrogative emanation somehow reached Otani. "That was Sakamoto. He's just had a message from the German Consulate General in Osaka," he explained. "They've had a call from Mrs Liebermann. It seems she's been staying with friends. She's going to see them tomorrow and they'll arrange for her to be available for Kimura to interview. Where *is* he, anyway?"

"You tell me," Noguchi suggested, and turned ponderously to the window.

"I wonder . . ." Otani began, then stopped himself and

started again. "Surely not . . . look, Ninja, are you really convinced?" Noguchi's shoulders moved a fraction of an inch, with the effect of a massive shrug. "I'll credit that this boy of yours says he recognises the photograph of Liebermann as the man who took him to his house that night, where he claims he found the gun. In fact it's an amazing stroke of luck, and we probably ought to go there with a search warrant and look round. It certainly seems to implicate Mrs Liebermann, too. But Liebermann a dealer?"

Noguchi shrugged again. "No use jumping to conclusions. Worth following up, though. This Liebermann supplies shooters, lot of money involved, gets across one of the *yakuza* bosses . . ." He clicked two fingers together with a dry snap. "Finish him off, looks like a heart attack. It's a theory."

Otani shook his head slowly. "Have you tried it on Kimura?"

"Not yet," Noguchi said. "Haven't seen him today."

Otani stood up and walked a few paces, then went back to his desk and perched on the edge of it. "I don't want to interfere," he said. "There's a dimension to all this that bothers me, though. It begins to look as if this German was a pretty unpleasant character and, if the boy is to be believed, a criminal of some kind. At the very least, open to be pulled in for corruption of minors. A man doesn't set up something like that lad described on the spur of the moment, and it seems to me that if he made a habit of hanging round discos and so on, then one of our undercover men ought to have noticed him. And if this new idea of yours is worth anything, he must have had a channel of communication to the *yakuza*. Pretty difficult to handle all that and still keep a clean record with us, let alone being apparently a fairly prominent figure among the businessmen in town."

Noguchi turned and looked at Otani with an expression of concern that was as impressive as it was uncharacteristic. "Some powerful friends he had. People like Maeda, didn't you say? Friend of yours too, old Maeda. Not worried about that, are you?"

Otani took a deep breath and nodded. "A bit, Ninja. More

than a friend. My old commander . . . I idolised him for years. I've never lost touch with him. I know he started in business with a lot of advantages, but all the same, he's really had an amazing career. I find it almost impossible to accept that he'd allow himself to get mixed up in anything shady. Especially with a character like the German. All the same, when I talked to him today he seemed to know a lot more about him than if he were just a casual acquaintance . . . and the wife. And he seemed very anxious to push the heart attack theory. I'd like very much to rule him out of this case, but I don't see how we can."

Noguchi continued to look at him. "Want some advice?" he asked. Otani remained silent. "Give you some anyway," he rumbled on. "Keep out of this one. Kimura's not the fool he looks. I'll talk to him. Anything points to Maeda, we'll let you know."

"Thank you, Ninja, but I don't think that's possible. Sakamoto's coming to see me in a few minutes, and I have a strong suspicion that he's going to make a formal complaint about Kimura's handling of the case. He's thoroughly put out that I didn't give it to him in the first place. I shall have to hear him out. I have a feeling that the only way I shall be able to shut him up will be to tell him that I'm taking personal charge of it." Otani stood up abruptly and squared his shoulders. "Quite apart from that, I hope I'm still capable of thinking rationally about Maeda or indeed anybody else I know. It's not as if he's a member of my own family. I agree, that *would* rule me out."

Noguchi stared at him in silence for a moment, then nodded slightly. "Have a word tomorrow then, shall we?" he said, and moved to the door.

"Yes, let's do that, Ninja. Oh, and when Kimura turns up, I want to see him."

"Thought you might," Noguchi said as he closed the door behind him.

Chapter 13

KIMURA PRETENDED TO LIKE WINE MORE THAN HE really did, and fussed over the list before deciding. Ilse Fischer accepted his offer of an aperitif, and chose Campari. Kimura followed suit, and they surveyed each other cautiously over the rims of their glasses after Kimura raised his in a perfunctory toast and they each sipped. Pleased and surprised by the amount he had discovered more or less inadvertently, he nevertheless considered that there was a chance of forcing Ilse to come clean, and pondered tactics as he picked at his plate of antipasto in a desultory way. It occurred to him that it resembled nothing so much as a complete Japanese dinner on a single plate, without the rice and pickles and not nearly so beautiful.

Ilse was lost in her own thoughts, and it was some minutes before she put her fork down and looked at Kimura. "Go ahead," she said almost plaintively in Japanese. "Ask me your questions now."

Kimura shook his head firmly. "No. Not until you've made some sort of sense of this afternoon's foolishness. After that, if I have questions I might very well put you under arrest and ask them formally, at police headquarters."

The hazel eyes widened and darkened, and Kimura had a

strong sense that she was willing him to say more, to revert to the amateur Lothario style in which he had first approached her. He found her disturbingly attractive with some of her defences down, but declined to oblige.

"I am a senior police officer investigating a case with some curious features, Fischer-san," he said grimly.

"It was Ilse a little while ago," she protested with a smile, but he brushed the remark aside, gesturing brusquely.

"I went along with your absurd play-acting today because I thought that as an intelligent woman you must have some good reason for it. I'm waiting to hear it."

Their waitress had been hovering uncertainly in their vicinity and now approached and timidly took their plates away, the tension of the atmosphere communicating itself to her. They both ignored the chicken breasts *fiorentina* which she brought immediately afterwards. Then Ilse lowered her eyes, not evasively but as though to concentrate, and spoke with quiet urgency. "Irmgard—Frau Liebermann—has been involved with Dangoro for the past year or so," she said, picking up a fork and tracing a hatchwork of lines on the white tablecloth as she spoke. "Richard knew about it but seemed not to mind. Irmgard would go away for days at a time, and he always told the neighbours she was visiting friends in Tokyo, or even on a shopping trip to Hong Kong and so on. As a matter of fact she was spending the time with Dangoro. He's not married, and of course he's not performing all the time. They often go away together. He is only famous in the *bunraku* world. When he is wearing ordinary clothes and using his real name, nobody imagines who he is."

Kimura suddenly became aware of the aroma emanating from his plate, cut a piece of chicken and chewed it thoughtfully. "This is quite good," he said after swallowing and drinking a mouthful of wine. "Does Dangoro know that Liebermann is dead?"

"That is what I was trying to find out," said Ilse.

Kimura took another mouthful and stared at her as he ate it. It was tiresome when foreigners told lies. The fact of it was usually obvious to him, but it was peculiarly difficult to work out what might be the truth which was being concealed.

Whatever Ilse Fischer had been saying to Dangoro, he was almost certain that it had not taken the form of questions. It had sounded much more as though she had been trying to persuade him of something.

"So," he said flatly. "And *did* you find out? Eat some chicken." He waved towards her untouched food and she looked at it, but still made no move to eat.

"Yesterday I thought Irmgard might be with him, so I rang him at the theatre. They had the same programme as today, and I was able to speak to him between performances. I said nothing about Richard and just told him I had an urgent message for Irmgard. But he said he hadn't seen her since before the holidays."

"You haven't answered my question," Kimura insisted.

Ilse looked at him vaguely, then her expression seemed to clear. "You mean whether he knows about Richard? Well, there has been nothing in the papers, has there? I didn't ask him directly today, but my impression was that he doesn't know."

Kimura pushed his plate away and snapped his fingers at the waitress. "Coffee," he commanded, then turned to Ilse. "You're not going to eat that, are you?" he asked. She shook her head and he told the girl to take the plates away, then leaned forward over the table on his elbows. "Two questions I will ask now," he said. "Straight answers, please. What did you say to Dangoro; and why the nonsense about who I was?"

He watched her as she replied, and this time could not have said whether or not she was telling the truth. "After I first talked to you at the office," she began slowly, "I thought hard about what you said. About Richard's death. You hinted that it wasn't what we thought, a heart attack. I wondered about it, and I thought that any police investigation would be certain to cause a lot of trouble for Irmgard and Dangoro. Then your men came to the office and started questioning everyone about where they were on Boys' Day, so you must have discovered something. You think Richard was killed, don't you?"

Kimura nodded very slowly. "Yes, we think so," he said.
120

She fell silent, and after a while Kimura got up, beckoned to her and made his way over to the cash desk to pay. One or two of the very grandest Western-style restaurants had adopted the weird and thoroughly un-Japanese practice of giving the waiter the bill to bring to the table. The Abela at Umeda was not one of them.

"I'll take you home," Kimura said when they were outside. "Hyogo Police will pay for a taxi." It was early enough in the evening to make it an easy matter to hail one, and the driver was pleased at the prospect of a good half-hour run terminating in another prosperous area. Kimura sat silently and not too close to Ilse for several minutes before resuming his questioning.

"All that absurd business about 'Bob Matsuda'," he said then. "I don't like being made to look ridiculous. You could perfectly well have introduced me without mentioning my job. I don't exactly look like a policeman, do I?"

Ilse looked at him from the dim shadows of the taxi. "Thank you for responding so marvellously," she said, then hesitated and pointed a warning finger at the driver. "Should we talk more later?"

"Uh? Oh, perhaps," said Kimura, mildly embarrassed by his want of discretion. In the restaurant there had been very little chance of being overheard. He could switch to English but even though the likelihood that the taxi driver would be able to understand was small, it was always just possible. He was irritated by the way the woman always seemed to manage to turn the subject when he put a straight question to her, and sat huffily in his corner for the remainder of the ride.

She lived in a small block of flats not far from the Ebisu shrine in the fashionable suburb of Nishinomiya, and a quick look at the array of bell-pushes beside the entry-phone speaker at the main entrance enabled Kimura to note with some surprise that Ilse was the only non-Japanese tenant. In his experience foreigners tended to develop little ghettos for themselves; but in this respect as in others Ilse was evidently a strange person. She appeared to take it for granted that he was to go inside with her, and after opening the glass door made straight for the stairs.

There were two flats on each floor and hers was on the second, with the name "FUISHA", in the squared phonetic script used for foreign words, on a neat card in a brass holder beside the bell. Ilse opened the door and again led the way, switching on lights as she went.

"Nice place you have here," Kimura said casually, his eyes flickering round the small living-room. It was really quite strange. The furniture was ordinary enough, the sort of thing one saw in any of the better-class department stores. It was the animals that were disconcerting. A huge stuffed Snoopy sat in one corner of the sofa, while at the desk against the far wall was a sizable teddy-bear dressed in what seemed to be a fisherman's outfit of yellow oilskins and rubber boots.

Smaller creatures were ranged on almost every horizontal surface, and they were all of the cute or cuddly variety. A fluffy black and white stuffed kitten peeped out of a man's hat upturned on an occasional table, while a big black velvet spider with a jolly smile was fixed so as to appear to be clinging to the edge of a Lufthansa calendar. There was an emerald green crocodile, a baby Dumbo elephant wearing a white sailor hat, and a comical snake with a bulbous red nose.

Ilse walked over to the sofa, and bemused as Kimura was by the decor he nevertheless had time to appreciate the roll of her hip movements as she walked and the brief view down the front of her dress as she bent to sit.

"Sit down, Kimura-san," she said. "A drink?"

"Later, perhaps," he said, shaking his head and sitting down in an armchair which gave him a good view of her face in the light from the table lamp at her side. It was without any doubt the face of a woman under strain; but Kimura found it impossible to make a more specific diagnosis.

The preoccupation which seemed to grip her unless she made positive efforts to control herself might have been due to grief, though this seemed improbable given the fact that everyone seemed in any case to have been expecting Liebermann to drop dead at any moment. Moreover, she had gone to the *bunraku* performance and sat through it, even if her main purpose had been to warn or consult Liebermann's widow, her lover or both. It was now abundantly clear that

122

she and Irmgard Liebermann were close friends, despite her earlier denials.

Perhaps, knowing that her employer had been killed, she was mentally running through a list of those who might have wished him dead. Perhaps she was herself the killer, and was pondering ways of diverting suspicion from herself; and perhaps again she was merely wondering how Kimura had come to include the puppet theatre in his sphere of investigation.

"Well, what do you want to know?" she asked after a silence in which she had clearly been waiting for Kimura to speak first. He was again struck by the easy fluency of her Japanese as compared with her stilted English.

"Everything," he said simply. "I meant what I said in the restaurant. I'll take you in for formal questioning if necessary, but that depends on how this conversation goes. Let's start with you. What you're like, why you don't seem to want to talk about the Liebermanns, how you got on with him, what you're going to do now your boss is dead, and so on. A lot more, but that will do for a start."

"How should I know what I'm like?" Ilse's manner was not so much defensive as bewildered. "Do you know what you're like? I'm complicated. So are you, I think. I don't mind talking about the Liebermanns if I must. As to how I got on with him—well, I worked for him. That's all. I am . . . not surprised that he is dead, but of course it is something of a shock. I must try to behave sensibly until a new manager can arrive."

Kimura settled into his working policeman's style. "Were you his mistress?" he asked in a brisk and businesslike manner.

A shutter seemed to come down over Ilse's face. "No," she said in a neutral voice. "Why should you think I might have been?"

"I'm sorry," said Kimura perfunctorily. "I shouldn't have put that to you so bluntly. Let me ask about Mrs Liebermann. If she's not with Dangoro, where do you think she might be? We really do have to get in touch with her."

Ilse shrugged her smooth shoulders. "I think she'll be back soon. She will be"—again an awkward hesitation—"distressed about Richard. But he was a difficult man, and they didn't get on well. She will get over it. She comes and goes.''

Kimura drummed his fingers on the arm of his chair, irritated by her consistent avoidance of simple answers to straight questions, uncharacteristic of other Westerners he had dealings with.

''Well, she will have a lot of questions to answer when she does appear,'' said Kimura. ''You realise that she is obviously under suspicion?''

Ilse had reached out a hand unconsciously and was stroking the Snoopy toy caressingly, as though it were a real puppy. Her eyes were dry but puffy, and she looked tired. ''I suppose so,'' she said slowly. ''And me too?''

Kimura nodded. ''Yes, I'm afraid so. I couldn't ask you this the day before yesterday, but now I want an answer. Where were you on Boys' Day?'' His stare bored into her, and she met it steadily.

''I was here,'' she said. ''I can't prove it. I had a lazy morning, and then of course there was the earthquake. There was clearing up to do.'' She stood up abruptly, and went to a drinks cupboard. ''Will you have something now?'' she asked.

Kimura nodded. ''Thank you. If you have some whisky?''

''I'll get some ice,'' she said, moving towards what must be the kitchen. Kimura stood up too. It was annoying: he should have gone at the restaurant.

''I, ah, may use your bathroom?'' he asked in his best American.

Ilse looked over her shoulder in astonishment as she replied in English. ''You want a *bath*? Oh, I see. You mean the WC—there, through the bedroom.'' She indicated another door and Kimura made his way through, slightly embarrassed. She pronounced ''WC'' in the German manner, and he had never heard it called a *vetsay* before.

There was only one stuffed animal in the bedroom; another teddy-bear perched in an easy chair. The bed was of a generous size and was made up as smoothly as if it were in a showroom. Kimura had been in a number of bedrooms belonging to European women in his time, and the lack of clutter in this one was striking. It was more like a spare room than anything, and he noticed the same severity about the bathroom as he used the lavatory.

After washing and drying his hands on a fluffy towel he looked into the bathroom cabinet and found very little beyond basics there. Only a throwaway plastic razor hinted at possible male use, but then she could perfectly well need that herself. On the way back through the bedroom Kimura opened the door of the built-in wardrobe and looked inside. Miss Fischer seemed to manage with a very modest collection of clothes, and only three pairs of shoes were lined up under the dresses in the hanging space. He would have liked to rummage further, but closed the door again after a few seconds and went back into the living-room, where Ilse handed him a tumbler containing ice and what looked like a very generous quantity of whisky.

"Thank you," he said, reverting to Japanese. "It's a good thing this isn't a formal official interview. If I drink all this I shall forget everything you say anyway." Ilse looked at him expressionlessly, then sat down, drank and put her own glass down. It looked like Campari again to Kimura, but he noticed an open gin bottle on top of the cupboard. She must have stiffened it to brace herself.

"Irmgard will need to give herself time to think about the future," she said suddenly, and Kimura nodded as he swallowed a mouthful of his whisky, which was indeed undiluted.

"Understandable. She might want to marry Dangoro, perhaps." A random thought struck him. "What about the dog? People become very fond of pets." He smiled and looked round the room. "Even stuffed toys. What about their dog?"

Ilse's face was still closed. Kimura watched her carefully but, beyond being convinced that she was thinking fast and weighing her words with care, could find no key to her feelings.

"The dog was one of the things they quarrelled about," she said after a while. "It was Richard's dog. He was crazy about it and took it everywhere except when he was planning a trip himself and couldn't take his precious Brumtzi with him. Then he insisted she should stay home.''

''Brumtzi? That is the Labrador's name? The Superintendent's driver will be glad to know,'' said Kimura.

Ilse nodded. ''Yes. Irmgard will be glad the Newfundländer—the Labrador you call him—is with the police. I can tell you one thing; she won't be wanting him back.''

Kimura raised an eyebrow. ''You seem very sure. When I first talked to you and asked you where Mrs Liebermann might be, you said you weren't a friend of the family.''

A spot of colour had appeared in Ilse's cheeks, and her eyes glittered. ''She never liked the dog. That's all.'' She picked up her glass again clumsily, and spilled a drop of the red mixture on her dress. ''Hell!'' She lifted the skirt to examine the stain, exposing a pair of elegant thighs, then dropped it again and met Kimura's eyes as he tore his gaze away. She seemed more confused than he, and to be covering the fact with more talk. ''If it comes to that, I didn't like it either. He took it to the office every day, and somebody had to take it out and walk it every morning and afternoon . . . and hairs everywhere . . . it seemed to be the only living thing he cared about . . .''

Her voice trailed off, and Kimura let the silence hang between them for a few seconds before shifting his position. ''Okay,'' he said then. ''If Mrs Liebermann wants to get rid of, ah, Betsy—'Brumtzi'—Brumtzi, and would like to give us a written authority, I suppose we can find a new owner, or have him put down.'' Ilse nodded, showing no regret at the possibility of the death of the dog, and Kimura decided to change the subject. ''Tell me more about yourself,'' he suggested. ''How did you learn your Japanese?''

''I can't read very much, and I can't write at all. Speaking and understanding isn't so difficult if you try,'' she said. ''When I knew I was coming here I borrowed a language course on records. And then I've always kept away from the Europeans here.''

Kimura was genuinely surprised. ''Really? You mean you don't go to the Kobe Club like all the others?'' Ilse shook her head firmly. ''Never. When I first arrived I had a few invitations from German families and so on, but I hate that kind of thing. You know, a single woman is always useful to make up a dinner party . . . or perhaps you don't." There was a faraway look in her eyes. "I always made excuses, and people soon forgot about me."

"You mean you have no friends among the foreigners *at all*?" Kimura enquired incredulously.

"No," she said simply. "Well, Richard of course. And Irmgard. I stayed at the Liebermanns' house for the first few weeks, until I found this place. It was convenient."

"What did Mrs Liebermann think about that?" asked Kimura. Like all Japanese he was conditioned to expect trouble with two women under one roof.

Ilse shrugged. "No problems," she said off-handedly.

Kimura sat back. "So much for not being a friend of the family," he felt moved to point out. "They seem to be the only friends you have."

Ilse looked surprised. "What a strange thing to say. I have a great many Japanese friends. Why come and live in a different country if you spend all your time among your own people?"

This stumped Kimura, who thoroughly enjoyed the society of foreigners himself and had few real friends among his own countrymen. He scratched his head and tried to put himself in her position. "I see what you mean," he said, with some reluctance. "So, how do you spend your leisure, then?"

Ilse looked down and rearranged the folds of her skirt demurely, then took a long drink from her glass, almost emptying it. "There's always plenty to do," she said. "Concerts in Osaka and Kyoto, films, theatre, festivals. That's why I learned Japanese, to be able to take care of myself." Another swallow, and the glass was empty. Her face was becoming pink, and she got up with a distinct effort and went back to the drinks cupboard. Kimura looked at his own glass which was still half full, and watched her splash a good deal of gin into hers before adding Campari and a lump of ice.

"You're obviously well known to the *bunraku* people yourself," said Kimura carefully, wondering why she was drinking so fast. "Was that through Mrs Liebermann?"

Ilse gazed at the sofa and drank yet again before replying. "Let's agree to call her Irmgard, shall we?" she said. "Yes. I go to the Asahi-za quite often."

"With Irmgard?"

Kimura's question seemed to amuse Ilse, whose taut expression relaxed into a wide, attractive smile accompanied by a creamy laugh fully worthy of her low-pitched speaking voice. "No, never. Never, never, never, Mister Policeman. Dangoro wouldn't like it. Finish your drink." Her face was now very flushed and she sat back and directed him an appraising look which Kimura found both intriguing and disconcerting as he drained his own glass. He prided himself on his head for liquor and was sure that he was still completely sober.

Then Ilse looked at a small wristwatch on a gold bracelet. "It's getting late," she said. "Do you have far to go?" The hint was as unsubtle as a blow to the head, and Kimura made to get up and go.

"No," he said. "My apartment isn't too far from here. But I must go." He stood, and looked down at her awkwardly. "I don't know whether to thank you or not. However, we'll meet again."

Ilse seemed to decide something, put down the glass she had been nursing and stood up. She continued in Japanese, easy, articulate and not only idiomatic but distinctly vulgar. "You don't have to go, Jiro," she said, startling him by the use of his first name. "I've seen the way you've been looking at me. Would it turn you on to screw your suspect?"

Kimura was at a loss for words in any language, and became simultaneously angry, confused and excited as she moved forward and kissed him hard, her arms snaking round his neck. His rational mind told him to resist, but then her hot wet tongue was probing and he felt himself stirring against her belly. Almost unconsciously he returned the kiss and put his arms round her body, feeling the smoothness of her back and the heavy soft pressure of her breasts.

The fact that she was his equal in height made it natural for his hands to move up over her shoulder blades to the base of her neck, and in the midst of his mounting involvement he
128

suddenly became aware of the fact. Ilse must have sensed the slight change in his response, because her mouth became softer and less urgent, and a few seconds later she broke off the kiss. She looked at him strangely. ''Are you going home, or are we going into the bedroom?'' she said, this time in English, which somehow emphasised the huskiness of her voice.

Looking at her, Kimura realised that he had just two options. The third, to ask her whether she had ever learned any judo, was really almost unthinkable. With an effort he pulled himself together and released her. One of the buttons of her dress was undone and he gently fastened it for her. ''I guess I'd better go,'' he replied in the same language. ''Not because I don't want you. I do, a lot. But I can't stop being a policeman until you're clear. Then, I'd like very much to be one of your Japanese friends.''

He smiled, bowed slightly and went to the door. Opening it, he smiled again, with something of an effort. Ilse was standing where he had left her, also smiling without apparent rancour. Indeed, he thought he detected a slight air of relief on her part which rather wounded his pride.

Chapter 14

"**I** NEVER HEARD OF ANYTHING SO RIDICULOUS IN MY life, even from you, Kimura," Otani snorted from the window of his office. It had been broken in the earthquake, but had been the first to be repaired, and Otani reached out and carefully removed a tendril of fresh putty with a fingernail, then cleaned off the small patch of discoloration with a paper handkerchief. His back was to Kimura, who was standing glumly at the other side of the room, one hand resting on the top of a metal filing-cabinet. The Gothic style of the reproduction of a Victorian painting hanging not far from his head matched the broody unhappiness of his face very well.

Kimura had offered only a severely edited account of his outing the previous day, and had omitted entirely any reference whatsoever to the final part of the evening, about which he still had a good deal of thinking to do. It was just as well: Otani had reacted with frosty displeasure to the news that he had been to and met Miss Fischer at the *bunraku* theatre, had been backstage with her and met two of the puppet masters, and had later given her dinner. In reassuring him that he had not been introduced as a police officer, Kimura dreaded to think what would happen if Otani ever discovered how he *had* been introduced.

Otani wheeled round and confronted Kimura. It was early afternoon, and he had been out all morning. "So all you discovered was that Mrs Liebermann was not in the company of this Dangoro person. And you can't be sure even of that. A grotesque waste of time, trouble and expense," he said quietly enough, but in the tight controlled voice which Kimura least liked to hear him use.

"Sir," he said humbly, taking his hand off the filing-cabinet. At least he was wearing a neat dark suit like Otani himself. "With respect, the connection with the puppet theatre is clearly important. Also, seeing her there convinced me that Miss Fischer is extremely important to this case and I felt obliged to see where she would lead me."

Otani marched over to his desk and sat down heavily. "Half way up Mount Fuji and back by the north coast road, by the sound of it. I had Sakamoto in here yesterday while you were wasting your time," he said in a slightly more relaxed manner. "If you had been at your desk, you would have received the message yourself."

"Message, sir? I've been with Ninja most of the morning. What message?"

"Sit down, Kimura. You look like a department store dummy standing there by the wall. And you're acting like one. I said Sakamoto gave *me* a message. From the German Consulate General. Mrs Liebermann telephoned, it seems."

Kimura sat down very slowly in the straight chair in front of Otani's desk. "Where from?" he said.

Otani opened his hands and raised both eyebrows, dislodging the heavy frames of his glasses. He reached up and readjusted them. "I don't know. From the home of the friends she's been staying with, I presume. Anyhow she'd heard about her husband's death. She sounded very distraught, according to the message from the Consulate. Asked them to start making the funeral arrangements on her behalf. There's been a further message. She went to see them this morning, in something of a state. The Consulate suggest that we should delay questioning her for a day or two."

He looked at Kimura sternly. "Frankly, Kimura, I was extremely angry yesterday. Sakamoto as good as asked me to

131

transfer the case to him, and I may say that I was very tempted to do so. Your so-called report this morning makes me regret that I did not.''

Kimura thought fast and furiously as he continued to look meekly at his hands. It was infuriating that he should have been out when the call came from the Germans, and even more maddening that it had been put through to Sakamoto instead of to his own deputy. However, it appeared that Otani had not in fact done as that miserable old devil Sakamoto had characteristically suggested.

''Sir,'' he said again. It had been months since he had been so formal with Otani. ''May I ask what you did decide to do?''

Otani sat back, much more in his habitual contained but approachable manner. ''I decided to take the case back under my personal supervision,'' he said, then unexpectedly smiled briefly at Kimura. ''Don't take it too hard, Kimura-kun,'' he said amiably enough. ''I don't want to give it to Sakamoto any more than you would have wanted me to. But it's not enough to chase about on a case. Someone has to be visibly in charge of it, and so far as anyone knew you might have disappeared off the face of the earth. You may or you may not have opened up a promising new line, but there are a great many other things to be done as well.''

He paused, and looked at a piece of paper he picked up from the desk in front of him. It skidded on the heavy sheet of glass, and his fingers skittered round in pursuit of it before they finally had it. ''I made a few notes. I authorised them to go ahead with the funeral, but told the police surgeon to get two more opinions on the cause of death before the body was handed over to the undertaker. They were obtained later yesterday, and confirmed that there was definitely an interruption of the blood supply through the carotid arteries. Then this morning I drafted a Press notice to the effect that we are investigating the circumstances of Mr Liebermann's death. That the possibility of criminal proceedings is not ruled out.'' He looked up.

''I did that at home before I set out, and took the draft to discuss with the District Prosecutor. He wants more time to think about it, but I think he'll agree it. We must obviously give the papers something. So far, so good.'' His eyes were fixed on Kimura's. ''We've worked together well enough many times before, Kimura-kun, so don't start getting touchy now.''

Kimura smiled ruefully. ''There is *one* other point that we've been following up, Chief,'' he said, trying his luck with the slangy form of address which sometimes amused Otani. The solemn expression on the Superintendent's face remained, but no actual rebuke followed.

''I said I spent the morning with Ninja. We drove out to the training centre, and had a long session with the chief judo instructor there. He confirmed what Ninja and I already knew. The strangles and choke-holds are almost always applied when the contestants are down on the mat, and the *hadaka-jime* isn't the preferred hold.''

''Naked strangle? That sounds as if it ought to be your preferred hold, Kimura-kun.'' Otani was grinning openly now, and Kimura realised that he was delighted at having been presented with a perfect excuse for giving himself an operational job again. There was nothing to be done but make the best of it, and try not to rise to this kind of bait.

''The phrase,'' he explained owlishly, ''implies simply that it is one of the holds which do not depend on grasping any part of the other person's clothing. I should have realised the other day that nearly all the so-called choke and strangle holds operate by rolling back the muscles that normally cover and protect the carotid arteries. With the *haduku-jime* the right forearm is locked round the opponent's neck with the left hand and the pressure can be applied to the back of his head with the attacker's own forehead or with his right shoulder. Unconsciousness can be produced in two or three seconds.''

''And death?'' said Otani, grasping his own right hand with his left and peering at Kimura over the top of his horizontal forearm. He had a very vague recollection of learning the hold in his remote youth, but had never been particularly good at feats of physical activity.

''Well, of course they always play down the dangers, and

in properly supervised judo training with strict courtesies it seldom goes beyond momentary dizziness. Like when Ninja grabbed me. But every black belt is taught the *katsu* resuscitation technique, and a bit about the killer holds.''

Otani found Kimura in this vein interesting and informative, and nodded encouragingly. ''Go on, Kimura-kun. And this is a killer hold?''

''The chief instructor hated talking about it,'' said Kimura with a smile of reminiscence. ''He's sixth *dan* and very good indeed. When you get to that stage you become a bit mystical about judo, and I had to remind him that I wanted information relevant to a murder case.'' He looked up. ''Yes, it can be a killer. Probably no more than ten seconds would be needed, and *katsu* would be ineffective after five or six.''

They looked at each other in silence for a few moments. ''What about applying it to a man in a sitting position? Practically impossible, surely?'' Otani asked in a tone which sounded almost pleading, like a child fearful of being deprived of a promised treat.

''Impossible if he offered any resistance,'' said Kimura meaningly, and Otani looked at him in some surprise.

''I have encountered some very odd things in my time,'' he said, ''but I find it hard to imagine Liebermann allowing someone to apply a judo stranglehold on him for ten full seconds. Unless,'' he added thoughtfully, ''he *wanted* to be killed. Suicide with an accomplice, to look like a heart attack? Insurance?'' Otani sat back running through his mind some of the familiar formulae of the *krimi* novels he liked to read. It was a positive pleasure after brooding over the puzzle of the Baron's apparent involvement.

Kimura was accustomed to these flights of fancy on the part of his chief, and invariably indulged them. ''Could be, Chief,'' he agreed. ''It gives us new possible leads to follow up. I have another suggestion.''

Otani blinked, giving Kimura no more than half his attention, then shook his head in irritation. ''No, that wouldn't do. He was obviously getting ready to do some dictation. Interrupted, obviously. Not consonant with assisted suicide.''

Kimura waited patiently till Otani broke off his musings,

then tried again. "The hold doesn't call for great physical strength, Chief," he said. "All the work is done by the head or shoulder. A woman could perfectly well apply it. And it only takes two or three seconds to induce unconsciousness. It could start off as a kind of embrace."

Otani sat up straight. "That's *very* good, Kimura-kun," he said. He pondered for a while, thinking about the many times Hanae came up behind him unobtrusively as he sat reading or watching television and gently massaged the muscles of his shoulders and neck. It was deliciously relaxing. He shuddered slightly as he briefly entertained and hurriedly dismissed the thought of Hanae's soft arms sliding round, and a sudden remorseless pressure on the back of his head.

"That points straight to Mrs Liebermann—or to your lady friend," he said almost accusingly to Kimura. "What sort of terms was he on with *her*, do you think?"

Kimura looked slightly uncomfortable. "I don't know, really, Chief," he admitted. "She didn't give me the impression of thinking much of him. I was planning to interview her again, ah, pretty soon."

Otani shook his head sadly. "Interview, interrogate, or take her out *at your own expense*?" he demanded. "There are differences, Kimura."

Kimura made no answer, and Otani decided not to press him for one. "We certainly need to know a good deal more about her relationship with Liebermann. And with Mrs Liebermann, for that matter. I want to be there myself when you question *that* lady," he said, then all at once realised that he was not necessarily on this occasion dependent on Kimura, as he tended automatically to assume where foreigners were involved. He pointed a minatory finger at Kimura. "They can *both* speak Japanese, didn't you say?" he demanded.

"Yes, but . . ." began Kimura, but Otani cut him off.

"Listen to me, Kimura-kun," he said. "There is no reason in the world why I should not interrogate these two German women myself. In Japanese."

Kimura put on a wooden, unhelpful expression. "They may refuse," he muttered.

Otani shrugged. "They may," he conceded, "but then

again they may not. I am willing to accept the German Consul General's request to leave Mrs Liebermann alone for a day or two but in return I see no reason why she should not co-operate in answering questions in our language, if she is capable of doing so. She is presumably having her love affair in Japanese.''

''No, German I expect,'' said Kimura absent-mindedly.

''What?''

''Dangoro speaks fluent German,'' he explained.

Otani brushed all this aside. ''Well, we shall see,'' he said, a touch of hauteur in his manner. He took off his glasses and twirled them round by one earpiece. ''Very well, Kimura,'' he said decisively. ''I won't interfere with your plans for Fischer-san. Whatever they are. I want you to make it clear to her, however, that she will be expected to present herself at this headquarters for formal questioning shortly. If she insists on using *her own* language an interpreter will be present. And that can't be you, Kimura,'' he added cunningly, and let a significant silence develop before continuing.

''Good,'' he then said. ''I think we understand each other. A good theory about the 'naked strangle', Kimura.'' He glanced at his open desk diary. ''We'll meet here tomorrow morning at ten, please.'' He nodded in dismissal and Kimura hesitated, then made for the door. ''Tell the people in your section where they can contact you this time, Kimura,'' Otani said as he went out, the iron back in his voice. ''Oh, and I would advise you not to turn your back on Fischer-san when you are next alone with her.'' Kimura banged the door, but not quite loudly enough for it to constitute a real impertinence, and Otani sat back, intrigued. The Case of the Naked Strangler? It sounded exactly right for a station bookstall.

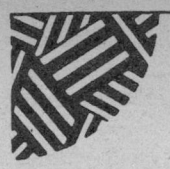

Chapter 15

HANAE WAS CONSTRUCTING A SPINACH SALAD WHEN SHE heard the car door slam shut and her husband's cheerful shout of "I'm home!" She hastily put down the neat cylindrical roll of lightly cooked leaves which she was cutting into one-inch lengths with a wickedly sharp knife, dried her hands and quickly pinched her cheeks before running to the porch, calling out as she went "Welcome home!" She had no need to try to make her eyes sparkle: they always did when Tetsuo came home, even after so many years.

Otani was already sitting on the step taking off his shoes, and Hanae sank to her knees not so much out of excessive courtesy as to bring their heads to a level.

"Are you tired?" she asked in the time-honoured words, and he smiled.

"Thanks to you, no," he replied conventionally. "And thanks to having the place to ourselves again," he added in a conspiratorial way, and Hanae wagged her head reprovingly, getting up and leading the way into the downstairs sitting-room.

"You're always complaining about how little we see of Akiko and Kazuo-chan. Then when they do all come and stay you can hardly wait to send them away again," she said, then gave a little squeak as Otani grabbed her round the waist and squeezed.

"I miss our nights of passion," he growled thunderously in her ear.

"You're *hurting*," said Hanae breathlessly but without conviction, and freed herself. Turning, she looked carefully at his face. It was fairly obvious that her equable, kindly husband was entering one of his rare manic moods. They could be exhilarating but were invariably exhausting.

"Something interesting has happened," she said, "hasn't it?"

"Tell you later," he said, pulling off his jacket and tossing it to the tatami matted floor. "First, a moment of sensual debauchery." He reached towards her, but Hanae fended him off.

"First, bath!" she corrected him firmly. He grinned.

"You come too," he suggested. She shook her head. It would never do to get flustered so early in the evening.

"Tonight you bathe alone," she said. "I'm busy cooking supper."

Otani pulled a face but simmered down slightly and made his way towards the bathroom, undressing as he went and leaving a trail of discarded garments behind him. "I'm sure Kimura doesn't have this sort of trouble with his women," Otani called hollowly from the little bathroom. Hanae ignored him, smiling quietly to herself as she patiently picked up the clothes from the floor and mounted the polished wooden stairs to put them away upstairs.

She then went back to the kitchen and finished chopping the spinach. The sesame seed and soy sauce dressing was already mixed. Hanae hesitated a moment, then cut two slices from a big apple, imported from Australia and bought at huge expense in the department store. Chopped quite fine it would give a little something extra to the salad. Hanae was checking the ginger sauce for the pork fillet when Otani appeared again, somewhat more moderate in his manner. He was wearing a fresh blue-patterned cotton *yukata* which clung to him damply, and his hair was plastered down, its wetness disguising to some extent the amount of grey in it.

138

Hanae looked him up and down. "You look nice, and you smell nice," she said with satisfaction.

"My back is probably filthy," he grumbled mildly. "You know I can't do it myself." He crossed over and opened the oven door.

"You shouldn't do that," said Hanae.

"Just peeping," he protested. "I'm glad it's pork. Oh, sorry. I left my lunch box on the porch. Hardly had time to eat properly today." Hanae pointed silently at the beautiful old lacquer box, already washed and dried. Sooner or later he would tell her about the day's events. There was no need to rush him.

She took off her apron and started to loosen the cord of her broad sash, then thought better of it and ducked neatly past Otani and out of the kitchen before he could intercept her. "I'm going to have my bath now," she said over her shoulder. "There's nothing to do in the kitchen for twenty minutes. Why don't you look at the paper or the TV? There's a bottle of beer in the refrigerator."

Otani was now properly dry, and he eased the folds of his *yukata* round him more comfortably, then went and found the bottle of beer and an opened packet of rice crackers which was also in the refrigerator. He took them with a glass back into the living-room and switched on the television. The Otanis had held out against the first great wave of colour, and he was now glad they had. Not only had the prices actually come down, but the model they had bought the previous year was much neater than those of earlier generations. Hanae had never been tempted to fiddle much with the controls, and he had almost overcome the temptation; only to backslide when Akiko and her husband had bought them a remote control gadget for New Year a few months before.

He now played with his toy, while working his way through the beer and crackers, lounging on one elbow on the tatami. With so many channels to choose from, one could generally find a news bulletin without too much trouble, but it was still rather early and there seemed to be nothing but cartoons and baseball. Otani enjoyed watching sumo wrestling, but baseball left him cold. Hanae returned to find him absorbed in Popeye and finishing the last of the beer.

She too was now wearing a light cotton *yukata*, and a touch of lipstick; and looked down at him affectionately from the doorway. "Whatever would the criminal classes think if they could see you now?" she enquired.

He sat up and switched off the set from the gadget in his hand. "They would think 'Otani is planning a master-stroke', that's what they would think. And they would be right," he answered loftily. "And they would think, 'see how the poor man's shrew of a wife deprives him of food to the point where he has to watch television lying down.' I'm hungry."

He scrambled to his feet and surveyed Hanae. "You look very nice too, madam. I shall enter you for the Young Nude Housewife competition on the late night television."

Hanae went slightly more pink and turned away. He definitely *was* in one of his moods. Perhaps a heavier meal than usual might help. "Come and sit down, supper's ready," she said and made for the kitchen. It would be simpler to eat there tonight. She had actually watched the Young Nude Housewife show once or twice out of curiosity, and had hardly known where to put her face as a succession of modestly dressed middle-class ladies sat in the studio with a male interviewer discussing the finer points of their own naked images projected from the set of pin-up pictures taken of them a few days previously. Nudity had never bothered Hanae, but she drew the line at televising Mrs Average for the whole Japanese nation to scrutinise.

Otani behaved himself reasonably well during supper, which Hanae was pleased to see he obviously enjoyed, demanding a second helping of the ginger pork and three bowls of rice. He teased her gently about her cookery class at the YWCA, and otherwise stuck to generalities until the end of the meal, when he was cutting neat pieces from another apple and crunching them up thoughtfully. "That was really delicious," he said. "Well, I had Kimura on the carpet this afternoon."

Hanae had half expected him to be in a cheerful frame of mind that evening, since he had announced in a zestful way

140

over breakfast that he had taken over the case of the murdered German from Kimura. He always became moody after any protracted period of uneventful administrative work, and cheered up markedly when involved in an investigation. Even the excitement of the earthquake had made him look two or three years younger and Hanae had been wondering how long he would be able to keep his hands off Kimura's case.

"Poor Kimura-san," she said with a little sniff. "Why is everything always his fault?"

Otani pointed his fruit-knife at her in mock menace. "Because when things go wrong it usually *is* his fault," he said. "I sometimes wonder why I don't get rid of him. He's conceited, irresponsible, unreliable and sometimes astonishingly stupid. If old Sakamoto were sitting in my chair, Kimura would be directing traffic in some little town in the north of the Prefecture. He's always telling me I indulge Kimura too much."

Hanae wrinkled her nose in displeasure. "I've never met Sakamoto-san," she said, "but he sounds awful. I *have* met Kimura-san, and I think he's very nice."

"Women generally do," said Otani gloomily. "That's the trouble. He can't keep away from them, and they encourage him. Oh, I like Kimura, you know that. He's amusing, and stimulating, and really very efficient when he's doing his proper job. He's a wonder with all those complicated regulations for foreigners. And he's good with foreigners . . . even seems to be able to think like them, sometimes. He's a very erratic detective, though."

Hanae very much wanted to ask what Kimura had done, but if she did there was a risk that her husband might change the subject. She sat quietly and looked at him with a completely neutral expression, and at first thought that her patience was rewarded.

"I really think he went off on the wrong track," Otani said after a while, almost to himself, then looked up at Hanae. "Evenings are very mild now," he said thoughtfully. "We shall have to start using anti-mosquito pads before long." Hanae nodded.

"Mr Kimura. Wrong track," she prompted gently, unable to resist the temptation.

He smiled. "Very well," he said, "you tell me. Here we have two German women, one of them missing until yesterday, the other one here. Now did Kimura concentrate on searching for the missing one, or did he go off to the theatre and see the one who *wasn't* missing, telling none of us where he was?"

Hanae nodded. "I see what you mean, but surely he must have had some good reason to go to the theatre. And then, I didn't think the other lady was actually *missing*. She was just away, wasn't she?"

Otani's expression remained patient and tolerant. "I don't think it makes much difference," he said. "We obviously needed to talk to Mrs Liebermann, and nobody seemed to know where she was. I call that *missing*. Anyway, she's back now, and the German authorities are taking care of everything for her. And taking care *of* her, I suppose. The poor woman must be having a difficult time. I expect one of the German officials will have her to stay. It must be strange for these foreigners at such times, thousands of miles from their families."

He looked slightly dreamy, and Hanae got up and cleared the table. Otani sat and watched her stacking the dishes at the sink, then got up and stood close behind her, slipping his arms round her waist, but gently and reflectively. Hanae nestled back against him contentedly, and made no attempt to stop him as he slid his hands up to cup her unconfined breasts. "Strange, isn't it," he said quietly, "to think that people can be on loving terms one minute, and then all at once one of them can actually get to the point of murdering the other?"

"Don't talk like that," murmured Hanae. "You make me feel quite frightened."

Otani kissed the nape of her neck where the black hair sprang out in silky wisps, and spun her round, putting his hands on her shoulders. He smiled at her. "I didn't mean us, Ha-chan," he said. Hanae relaxed. There was never any tension between them when he called her that. "As a matter of fact, I frightened myself a little this afternoon by realising

142

how easy it is for a person to kill another. Especially if that other person is very trusting." He looked at her for a long moment then gave her a huge hug, reverting to his earlier zany manner.

"In the meantime, woman, I'm playing detective again, and we sleuths need a lot of sex. Come to bed," he commanded. This time Hanae did as she was told.

Chapter 16

THE TRAFFIC IN THE DISTANCE PRODUCED NO MORE THAN a generalised rumble, and although the lights of the city centre illuminated the night sky behind them, Constable Migishima found his consciousness becoming dominated by two sounds; that of the lapping of the black wavelets against the lighters tied to the jetty, and the creaking of the ropes that made them fast. Had he been a more imaginative man he might have thought he could hear the beating of his own heart. He was quite nervous enough.

Beside him in the gloom Ninja Noguchi shifted from one foot to the other, then all at once cleared his throat and spat noisily into the sea. He was dressed much as on the previous occasions that Migishima had seen him, and although the visit to the Hochmuth-Wasserman wharf was at his suggestion, Migishima thought he was displaying singularly little interest in the proceedings.

Migishima had kitted himself out in the gear that struck him as appropriate: a dark sweater, jeans and rubber-soled shoes. He had asked Noguchi whether he should bring his police pistol, and the old bruiser had seemed genuinely shocked. "Heavens no, son. Don't want anything like that. Just going to have a bit of a look around," he had said after startling Migishima out of his wits by materialising behind him in Otani's ante-room when he was tidying up after saluting the Superintendent smartly on his departure for home.

Migishima had been much too absorbed by the comings and goings centring on Otani's office in the past two or three days to do more than smart occasionally at the recollection of the dressing-down Noguchi had given him in that very room on the morning of Boys' Day, and it had taken some time for it to sink in that Noguchi was inviting him to show him where they had found Liebermann's body. Since he stood in roughly equal awe of both Otani and Noguchi, he had dithered helplessly, till Noguchi had shown his mouthful of yellowing teeth in what was intended as an amiable grin and pointed out that the Superintendent would not be wanting him before the following morning, that he was inviting Migishima to go for a little off-duty walk in plain clothes and, conclusively, that he, Noguchi, would answer for it to the Superintendent if necessary.

That had been just after six, and it was now nearly ten. Their rendezvous had been for nine at the side of the custom house, giving Migishima time to go home and change as well as to frighten and impress his mother and younger brother with a few dark remarks about a special assignment. He had arrived much too early, and had been obliged to take evasive action when a uniformed policeman on patrol duty had looked him up and down suspiciously. Although Prefectural Headquarters was practically in dockland, the harbour itself was policed from a divisional office which also provided a small waterborne force, and Migishima had never seen this particular colleague before. It had been a relief when Noguchi's short but bulky and infinitely reassuring form had loomed up beside him in the shadows and they set off along the waterfront.

"I am sure you knew the way to this wharf, sir," Migishima whispered tentatively as Noguchi still stood at the water's edge, staring apparently aimlessly out towards the Inland Sea.

"Of course. Been down here a couple of times since the quake." The reply was curt and unhelpful.

Migishima tried again. "May I ask you why you need me

145

tonight, sir?'' Noguchi turned and surveyed him. The young man was a head taller than himself and he stabbed him with a hard forefinger at the base of the breastbone. It was quite painful.

"Because you were very lucky the other day, young man," he said. "You and the Superintendent were first on the scene after a murder. I want you to show me exactly where and how he was sitting. This Liebermann."

Migishima was aghast. "You mean . . . go in?" he stammered.

"Well, I haven't got X-ray eyes, you young idiot," Noguchi growled, and began to walk towards the warehouse and office block.

Migishima trailed behind. "But, sir," he protested, "what about alarms? Maybe there's a night security man . . ." The offices were not in total darkness, though the warehouse was. A single window on the first floor was illuminated, though dimly. Noguchi stopped in exasperation.

"Don't you read any of the reports you put in the Commander's in-tray?" he demanded. "If they had a security watchman he'd have been on duty on Boys' Day, right? And Inspector Kimura's report on the interviews with the staff here made it quite clear they only have a doorkeeper for the warehouse in working hours. Look."

Noguchi pointed up towards the top of the four-storey block. The display sign with the firm's name had been re-fixed, and a number of broken windows on the top floor roughly boarded up, like the shattered panel beside the main entrance. An alarm bell was prominently mounted on the wall at second-floor level, a ladder propped up beside it. Wires trailed from the bell casing, which looked new. "They're fixing a new system," said Noguchi. "It'll be wired to the central port security switchboard. Never bothered with one before. Inspector Kimura told them he thought they were crazy. Come on."

He made for the main entrance. The door was of heavy metal, and had a massive lock. Noguchi studied it judiciously. "Maybe one of Kimura's boys had the wit to make a note of the lock number," he said thoughtfully. "Should have checked." He shook his head. "Take too much to bother with this," he grunted. "Fire escape, son." He seemed to disappear before Migishima's startled eyes, and a few seconds later Migishima heard an irate undertone from the side of the building. "Get a move on!"

He hastened round and into a narrow passage between the office block and the warehouse, which itself abutted directly on to the western boundary fence with its frill of barbed wire. There was another concrete fence a few feet behind both buildings, and Migishima saw Noguchi in silhouette marching steadfastly up to the flat roof of the offices. The warehouse, being a single storey construction with its loading bay at the front, had nothing more than a simple door at the back opening on to four concrete steps to the ground.

Noguchi seemed to take the four flights of stairs with no trouble, but Migishima himself was slightly out of breath when he joined him on the roof after having to sprint up them to catch him. The view was impressive, even though they were only about forty feet up. The whole harbour opened up like a panorama, the red, green and white riding lights of a dozen or more merchant ships dipping gently. One or two were brightly illuminated as unloading was proceeding, and Migishima could see one fair-sized passenger liner moored to the "tourist" pier, number four, near the customs sheds. Farther out a late ferry was coming in from the direction of Shikoku Island.

"Finished gawping?" said Noguchi, but not unkindly. "We could always transfer you to the Port Division if you like. Hold this light for me." He was pointing the narrow beam of a pen torch at the simple cylinder lock of the door in the hutch-like excrescence which gave access to the roof from inside the building, and Migishima hastened to take the torch from him as Noguchi produced a bunch of keys from one sagging pocket of his jacket. There were perhaps twenty or so on the ring, and Noguchi looked through them, grunting to himself as he did so.

The fourth one he tried fitted the lock, and the door opened outwards. Noguchi stood back and beckoned to Migishima. "Down you go, lad," he said. "No need to make a racket."

Migishima gulped and stepped inside. His appreciation of the harbour lights had dulled his night vision, and his first impression was one of pitch darkness. He felt his way down the narrow wooden staircase, and it was not until he reached the top landing that he became aware of the faint source of light from below.

He heard Noguchi's footsteps behind him, and waited. "What now, sir?" he whispered. Noguchi said nothing, but shoved him in the back; Migishima stumbled forward and made his way down the slightly broader staircase to the third floor.

It was a good deal easier now. His eyes again became adjusted to the darkness, and more light filtered up from downstairs. Then Noguchi muttered in his ear. "Right down, son. We'll just check that light first, then you can show me the room where you found him." Migishima continued on down until he felt carpeting underfoot, and recognised the panelled doors at the bottom of the flight. The light was coming from the room next to Liebermann's and Migishima hesitated outside.

Noguchi pushed past him and applied an eye to the crack, then opened the door. There was nobody in the office, and the light came from a small reading lamp on the desk. "Whose office is this?" Noguchi asked, still quietly but in more normal tones.

Migishima peered over his shoulder. "I don't know," he said. "We found the body in this one." He gestured towards the second room.

Noguchi opened the door wide, so that the light gave him a better view of the landing and the second door. "This is the room you sealed? Right, let's have a look." The door was not locked, and Noguchi went in. Enough light came from the landing and from the obstructed windows for Migishima to be able to see quite well. It seemed extraordinary to him that only a few days had elapsed since he had first been in there.

"Kimura's people have already checked on all the papers, and a fingerprint man went over the room before it was handed back," said Noguchi in a conversational way. "Sit down, Migishima. Show me how he looked.'' Migishima crossed to the desk and sat down uneasily on the edge of the padded swivel chair before settling himself properly in the seat and slumping forward. Trying to remember Liebermann's precise position, he laid his head on the blotter, then arranged his arms as accurately as he could recall. It felt very odd but surprisingly comfortable, though he experienced a mounting sense of foolishness as he heard Noguchi prowl round the desk saying nothing.

''This is as nearly as I can remember, sir,'' he said in a muffled voice. ''May I sit up now?''

Noguchi grunted assent. His voice came from behind Migishima. ''Right, lad. Pretend to be using a dictating machine.'' Migishima positioned himself in what he judged to be the most appropriate way, and gazed at the glass doors of the old-fashioned bookcase facing him. ''Right. No need to be scared. I'm an old friend of yours,'' said Noguchi, and Migishima felt a companionable pat on his shoulder. Noguchi's other hand came down on the left side, and Migishima felt strong fingers probing and massaging the tendons of his neck. ''Don't worry, son, I'm not going to strangle you,'' Noguchi murmured.

Migishima's heart thudded with apprehension. It was all very well to assist in reconstruction, but nobody in Headquarters knew they were there, and Inspector Noguchi was a very eccentric sort of man. And very strong. Migishima stiffened as the hand moved, then relaxed again as Noguchi stood back. ''No good. Too awkward,'' he said to himself. ''Stand up, Migishima.'' The young man did so, and Noguchi pulled the chair clear and moved in behind him. Migishima had time only to feel his legs crumple and to clutch helplessly at the edge of the desk before an awful pressure closed in on his head and neck.

He came to in a matter of seconds, neatly rearranged in the slumped position he had himself previously adopted, and raised himself groggily to meet Noguchi's inscrutable gaze. A sense of outrage fought with a wave of relief, and he struggled to his feet and blinked a few times. ''Good. Well done, lad,'' said Noguchi affably. ''Sorry about that, but you took it better than Kimura, I must say. Big fellow, wasn't he? Lie-bermann.''

Himself again, Migishima tried to remember. He croaked a little at first, but rapidly recovered. "A fairly heavy man, sir. About my height, I suppose." Noguchi nodded, his face craggy and shadowed like the surface of the moon in the dim light.

"Well, it can be done. A shorter person can apply the hold, but only as the other one goes down. It was tricky but not all that much of a problem to get you back in the chair. All right, let's go home.''

He turned to the door. Migishima took a step, then froze. "Sir," he whispered. "There's a car coming." Even as he spoke the reflection of the sidelights in the bookcase glass disappeared, and they both heard the quiet crunch of tyres outside the building. There was a pause, then again the sound of the tyres and the whisper of the engine. "He's turning," said Noguchi, moving towards the window. "Expensive car, by the sound of it.''

Migishima had not moved, and this time it was the red of the rear lights which was momentarily reflected in the glass. Noguchi's head was cocked to one side as he stood in the shadows beside the window. "Stopped," he said after a while. "I was too late to get the number as it went by. Prob-ably a couple finding a quiet place to park for a comfortable hour. Too mean to pay for a short-time hotel." He led the way up the stairs. "We'll have a look from the roof on the way out," he was saying as there came the sound of a key in a lock, and Noguchi whirled round, a warning hand on Migi-shima's arm.

They heard the dull thud as the heavy front door was closed, and the sound of footsteps on the concrete of the ground floor. Noguchi very slowly sat down on the stairs, pulling Migishima down as well. Migishima felt a wave of excitement sweep through him and found it hard to keep still. Any moment now the intruder would come up the stairs, and at a signal from Noguchi he would fling himself down on him.

It was not to be. The footsteps came no nearer, but Migi-shima heard what sounded like the opening and shutting of a drawer, the clink of metal against metal, and then to his consternation the rattle of the main door handle again, followed a second or two later by the thud of the closing door. Noguchi remained immobile for several seconds, then leaned forward. "Roof," he said, and stood up. Migishima followed, and nothing more was said until they were again on the roof within the shadow of the access doorway.

"What do you make of it, lad?" he murmured to Migishima, who was completely at a loss.

"Somebody belonging to the staff here? Coming back to fetch something he left behind?" he hazarded.

"Keep your voice down," Noguchi breathed. "I think he's in the warehouse. Went to the office to get the key." He made the smallest sound of irritation. "Don't know whether to disturb him or wait till he comes out," he muttered. "All depends whether he's collecting or delivering."

He put his head very close to Migishima's. "Go down those stairs as quietly as you know how. If you see anyone, freeze. If you don't, make your way round to the front and note the car number if you can see it." Noguchi seized Migishima's wrist and looked at his watch. "About ten twenty-five. Meet me in five minutes by the jetty. I'm the night-watchman from the next wharf."

When Migishima next saw him, he looked it. After waiting in the shadow of the boundary wall by the jetty for a full ten minutes he saw a slender figure emerge from between the buildings and stroll unconcernedly up to the main entrance, open the door and go in, to emerge again a minute or two later and approach the car which was parked at the side of the approach road. He saw the stranger stop in surprise as Noguchi shuffled out of the shadows and greeted him with a kind of servile querulousness. Migishima could not quite make out what he said, but watched in admiration as Noguchi's manner changed from suspicious belligerence to a mollified affability, culminating in a scruffy half-salute as he opened the car door for the stranger and a gesture of gratified surprise as money obviously changed hands.

The car started, its lights blazed into life and it was gone. Migishima walked out of his concealment and went to join

Noguchi, who acknowledged him with a good-humoured nod. "Quite a gentleman," he said. "Five thousand yen for holding the door open. I'll buy you a beer, Migishima. Do your throat good."

Migishima could bear it no longer. "Who was it, sir? Did you recognise him?"

Noguchi looked at him. "Keep it under your hat, son," he said, "but I think I did."

Chapter 17

"**S**IT DOWN, GENTLEMEN," SAID OTANI BRISKLY AS Kimura and Noguchi entered his office from the ante-room. Migishima hovered in the doorway in an agony of expectation. The two inspectors made for the easy chairs in their regimented positions round the low table on which was a cloisonné enamel cigarette-box from Kyoto, with nothing in it, an ashtray prominently marked with the name of the Hakushika Sake Brewing Company, and a copy of the *Kobe Shimbun* newspaper.

Otani got up from his desk to join them. He was in uniform, and looked formidable and efficient. He noticed Migishima half in and half out of the room and nodded curtly. "Thank you, Constable," he said in dismissal, and Migishima's face fell.

"Can he stay?" Noguchi asked casually as he lowered himself into his chair. Otani stopped in his tracks, and Kimura looked up interestedly from an examination of his fingernails.

"What was that, Ninja?" Otani's tone was not encouraging. Noguchi was perfectly at ease.

"That young fellow. Migishima. Be useful if he could sit in on this."

Otani glared from one to the other. A fine start to a meeting at which he fully intended to assert his role as officer in charge. "Out!" he barked at Migishima, then, catching a glint in Noguchi's eye, continued in more level tones, "for the moment. While I speak to Inspector Noguchi."

The door closed behind Migishima, and Otani continued towards his own easy chair and settled himself into it. "I don't require a note of this meeting, Ninja, and what I have to say is confidential." Otani could not remember the last time he had been annoyed with Noguchi. It was not a pleasant sensation. At least Kimura was keeping sensibly quiet for a change. He was also turning up for work dressed in a reasonably unobtrusive way lately, though that would be unlikely to last.

Ninja Noguchi met his superior's bleak stare with a face which gave nothing away. "All right," he said. "I'd still like him in later. When I say my piece." Otani had not expected Noguchi to have a piece to say, and was thrown off balance. It had always in the past proved to be prudent to act on his advice, which was seldom volunteered. He looked from one to the other of his two closest associates, crossed one blue-grey uniformed leg over the other and addressed the air between them.

"We'll discuss it in a moment, Ninja," he said, still irritated but managing with an effort to achieve his usual manner. "Let me tell you both first what I hope to discuss this morning. Basically, I want to bring some order and system into an investigation which began in a confused way and which hasn't yet been considered as a whole." He became momentarily conciliatory. "I'm not blaming anyone. Not really." He glanced at Kimura, then again aimed his words between them.

"It was pure chance that I stumbled on the body of the German. He would have been found sooner or later, and there might or might not have been an investigation. Quite a few people died on Boys' Day. We've assumed that they were all victims of the earthquake, but we don't *know* that none of the others was murdered."

154

Kimura looked up. "Ninety-nine people out of a hundred would have taken it for granted that Liebermann had a heart attack," he said. "It took somebody of your experience to notice anything amiss." Otani was by no means averse to flattery, but almost invariably suspected Kimura's motives. He looked sharply at him, but there was nothing but judicious reasonableness in his face.

"Perhaps," Otani conceded. "Also a pathologist with his wits about him. Anyway, I found him and I discussed the case at its early stages with both of you, and gave it to Kimura. I know you talked about it between yourselves, especially the judo angle. Very sensible. Then Sakamoto became involved, for reasons which I needn't go into now." Another quick glance at Kimura. "Sakamoto wanted to take over. That would not have been a good idea. I took the case back myself, and I now intend to see it through. Obviously I can't do it without your help, and I shall rely on you both as always. And of course the routine support of Kimura's people, mainly."

He paused, and stood up, then crossed to his desk and fetched a clipboard with a few sheets of paper attached to it. "I regard it as being of the first importance," he said as he settled back into his chair and took a ballpoint pen from his tunic pocket, "to see that all aspects of the investigation are properly co-ordinated. We all have plenty of other work to do besides this case. So today I want to draw up a summary of what we all know between us, and what action needs to be taken. Then we may be justified in throwing a few theories about. Agreed?"

Noguchi and Kimura nodded. Otani turned to Noguchi and spoke to him directly. "Now, Ninja, I'm sure you can see that I hardly wanted that young constable to hear about the untidy way this case has been handled so far. I've said all I want to say about that, though. Tell me why you want him in here."

Noguchi was in his habitually crumpled state, but his baggy linen jacket was at least clean, and he appeared to have shaved more conclusively than usual. He scratched his battered nose reflectively. "You were right," he said, nodding fractionally. "No need for the boy to get disillusioned just yet. Might as well get the next bit over before he comes in, too."

"Next bit?" Otani had been congratulating himself on achieving a rational, comradely atmosphere. It seemed barely credible, but Noguchi gave the very slightest impression of being embarrassed.

Noguchi cleared his throat noisily, then seemed to refrain from spitting. "Yes, well," he growled. "I went down there with young Migishima last night. To the wharf."

Otani remained grimly silent, but Kimura was jolted out of his carefully controlled silence. "You *what*?" he squawked.

Noguchi looked at him balefully, then turned back to Otani. "The session with the judo king got me thinking. Wanted to try a reconstruction. I asked Migishima to show me where he'd seen the German. I told him I'd square it with you. Anyway, it turned out to be a very good thing we were there."

Noguchi fell silent, his bullet head descending even further than usual into his burly shoulders. Kimura's mouth was opening and shutting like that of a fish, before he found speech. "You . . . you took that constable there to poke your nose into my case, *without telling me*?" He was spluttering with outrage, and presented so comical a spectacle that Otani's own anger subsided a little.

"It wasn't your case last night, Kimura," he pointed out. "Let us get a few things clear. You should be the last person to complain about being in the dark. We shouldn't have found ourselves in this muddle if you'd stuck to the proper procedures. If there's to be any complaint about Ninja, it will come from *me*."

Kimura subsided rebelliously, and Otani turned to Noguchi. "It's not at all like you to do a thing like that," he said quietly. "You know I never enquire into your own movements. But Migishima is temporarily working for me personally. I should be obliged if you would first clear with me any future plans you may have involving him." The rebuke was as powerful in its effect as it was mild in its expression. Noguchi was after all older than Otani, and for him to be crit-

156

icised in the presence of an even younger man was galling in the extreme. He said not a word, and remained as still as a rock in a temple garden.

Even Kimura, who sometimes felt that he spent most of his working life being either teased or reprimanded by Otani, was moved to speak in Noguchi's defence. "Sir," he said tentatively, "a reconstruction would have been very useful anyway, and Migishima was the obvious person to do it. And Ninja said it was a good thing they were there . . ." His voice trailed off uncertainly, but broke the tension in the room.

Ninja Noguchi looked across at Kimura, and his mouth twitched. "Thanks, Kimura-kun," he said. "The Superintendent's right, though. I shouldn't take leaves out of your book." This brought a smile all round, and Noguchi perked up.

Otani tried to make amends. It was pointless to make a big issue of the matter, especially with Noguchi. "Well, it's over and done with, and Migishima is an important witness by any reckoning." He looked round. "Unless there are any other irregularities best kept to ourselves, I'm agreeable to having the Constable in. It might help us all to keep to the point." He looked quizzically at Kimura, who was making a mental inventory of his own irregularities, but remained silent.

Otani crossed to the communicating door and opened it, half expecting Migishima to fall in as people always did in films. In fact the young man was sitting stiffly at his small desk, ostentatiously reading a handbook of police procedure. He jumped to his feet as the door opened and came rigidly to attention. "I'd like you to join us, Migishima," Otani said mildly. "Inspector Noguchi tells me you were very helpful to him yesterday evening. We haven't heard the details yet." He nodded and half turned away, then spoke again over his shoulder. "I think we'd all like some tea, please. Bring a cup for yourself." He went back to his chair. "I'm sorry I've nothing stronger to offer you, Ninja," he said in an amiable voice.

Otani's normally easy relationship with his immediate subordinates had taken years to develop, and his manner towards more junior police officers was invariably courteous,

157

but formal and generally distant. Until Migishima had burst upon his awareness on Boys' Day it was only his driver Tomita among the rank and file who had been admitted to anything amounting to a private confidence. The curious events of the day of the earthquake had greatly accelerated what would otherwise have been a very long-drawn-out process, and Otani found it difficult to be stiff with Migishima. He was still too conscious of the episode of the carp streamers; and in any event the boy's coltish awkwardness and enthusiasm had an engaging quality.

Migishima now came in with the usual old tin tray and tea kettle and bashfully placed it on the table between the three senior officers. He had done as he was bidden and brought four of the plain brown handleless cups from Otani's set of five, and now filled three of them from the kettle. Otani sniffed appreciatively as the aromatic steam rose, then looked up at the tall young man, who stood timidly with the kettle in one large hand. "Sit down, Constable," he said. "Pour a cup for yourself."

Having reconciled himself painfully to being excluded from the charmed circle, Migishima was overcome at being admitted after all, and balanced himself on the very edge of the fourth chair round the table. He was much taller than any of the three older men, and by sitting bolt upright loomed over them impressively. Noguchi cocked an eye at him, his customary good humour apparently restored. "Relax, son," he said; and Migishima wormed his way backwards inch by inch into the chair and gradually unbent into a more reasonable posture.

Otani picked up his cup and sipped with pleasure, closing his eyes momentarily. Then he opened them again, took a second sip and nursed the cup on his knee as he began to speak. His clipboard for notes was balanced on the arm of his chair under his elbow. He looked at Migishima. "I want you to listen carefully, Migishima," he said. "We are about to review the Liebermann case, see if we can arrive at any preliminary conclusions, and decide on future action. I think," he continued, putting his cup down and passing the clipboard across, "that I shall ask you to make a note of the salient

158

points of the discussion. You should feel free to contribute to it where you have personal knowledge. And of course to offer suggestions if you have any."

Awed, Migishima took the clipboard and rummaged in his pocket for a pencil. Otani's ballpoint was lying on the table, but he lacked the confidence to reach for it. Otani leaned back and closed his eyes. Whatever his feelings about the reason for the young man's presence at the conference, to be in an expository role with a tutorial element in it did concentrate the mind most effectively.

"We begin with the facts. Facts which were either forced upon our attention, or which have come to light through a process of enquiry. We will try to avoid inferences at this stage," he said, and opened his eyes to see Migishima scribbling furiously, Kimura giving his polite attention, and Noguchi seemingly asleep. This was his normal attitude during conferences, and Otani was unperturbed. "No need to write that down, Migishima," he said with a touch of amusement, and the young man flushed and stopped writing. "You can start now." He took his glasses off and rubbed his eyes.

"Very well, gentlemen. Migishima and I discovered the body of a foreigner subsequently identified as Richard Liebermann, manager of the Japanese branch of the Hochmuth-Wassermann trading company. Having some reservations about the circumstances, I gave instructions for an autopsy, which suggested that Liebermann had not, as might have been thought, died from a heart attack brought about by the shock of the earthquake. Death from this cause might easily have come about, however, as the medical record held by the American doctor in Kobe indicates."

Otani raised a hand and ticked off points on his fingers as he continued. "Inspector Kimura and his staff conducted a routine interrogation of the fourteen Japanese employees, none of whom had been on duty for several days, because of Golden Week. Liebermann had given them all time off for the whole period, not only the public holidays but also the intervening working days. There is no permanent watchman, but Liebermann told Sakai, the senior Japanese employee, that he or his secretary Miss Ilse Fischer would check the premises from time to time. There was no permanent security man nor, surprisingly, any burglar alarm. Sakai explained that there was seldom much of value on the premises except on payday each month and at bonus time each June and December, and then hardly a fortune. Is that right, Kimura?''

Kimura nodded. ''Yes. I asked him myself about the warehouse. They were holding a fair amount in the way of stocks, but it was all enormously heavy stuff and in any case virtually useless from the point of view of thieves. The bearings nearly all go to heavy industry here on a regular contract basis. The lighter at the jetty has a consignment on board, in sealed metal containers. Casual burglars would be unlikely to bring a crane operator and heavy truck to steal them.''

Otani nodded and continued. ''The first difficulty arose when it proved impossible to make contact with Liebermann's wife on the evening of the day in question, Boys' Day, 5 May. Not surprising, on the day of a major earthquake. The German Consulate General was duly notified on the following day, but were also unable to get in touch with her until the day before yesterday, by which time we had confirmation that Liebermann had not died from natural causes. A Press statement has been issued, and we must presume that that fact is now widely known.'' He pointed towards the table. ''It's in today's *Kobe Shimbun*.

''Inspector Kimura has had discussions with staff of the German Consulate General, and with Miss Fischer. We have agreed to defer an interview with the widow until after the funeral, which is to be tomorrow.'' Otani picked up his teacup again and drained it, then reached forward for the kettle, but Migishima was ahead of him and refilled the cup for him. ''Inspector Kimura will now report such facts as have emerged from his discussions with Miss Fischer,'' he said with the slightest possible emphasis on the word ''facts''.

Noguchi opened one eye and surveyed Kimura, but otherwise remained motionless. Kimura sat up and placed the tips of his fingers together judiciously. ''I have seen Miss Fischer on two occasions,'' he said formally. ''First in her office on the afternoon of 6 May, and then again on Tuesday the 8th. The first meeting was a formal interview, but conducted before we had an authoritative opinion on the cause of death; and the second was . . . accidental.'' He looked at Otani. ''I wonder, sir, if it would be appropriate to discuss the evidence represented by the articles removed from the man's body?''

Otani shook his head. ''Later, please, Inspector. We will note though that among those articles was a single ticket for a *bunraku* puppet performance in Osaka on the afternoon of the 8th, and that you made use of this ticket.''

Kimura cleared his throat and began again. ''I saw Miss Fischer arrive at the Asahi-za Theatre, and after keeping her under observation for the first part of the performance I approached her and was introduced by her to two of the puppeteers. Following the performance I questioned her at length.'' He paused, then continued, his eyes piously upraised towards the ceiling, which was badly cracked and would need extensive repairs and redecoration. ''At a restaurant and subsequently at her flat.''

He coughed. ''So far as facts are concerned, it should be noted that Miss Fischer is a part-time employee of the Hochmuth-Wassermann firm, even though she entered the company on a full foreigner's work permit. She speaks fluent and idiomatic Japanese.'' Otani was watching him closely and could have sworn that Kimura began to blush before quickly going on. ''She lives alone, and asserts that she has no friends or acquaintances among the European community here; except for Mr and Mrs Liebermann, with whom she lived for a time. I think it is a fact that she is under a good deal of strain and that she has consistently lied or withheld the truth from me. The rest is speculation.''

''Have you noted that, Migishima?''

''Sir!'' the young man said smartly, clearly beginning to enjoy his appointed role.

''Good. Now I should report a conversation I had with Bunsho Maeda, former President of the Maeda Trading Company,'' said Otani. Once more Noguchi opened one eye and then closed it again.

''Maeda-san is an old acquaintance of mine, and I saw him at my Rotary Club on Tuesday. He is Chairman of the Chamber of Commerce this year. Liebermann was one of a small number of foreign members, and Maeda knew him well. He is also on friendly terms with Mrs Liebermann. He confirmed to me that Mrs Liebermann is widely known to be having a love affair with one of the *bunraku* puppeteers. There is a further connection: Maeda is on the board of the *bunraku* company. He also knew that Liebermann was in poor health and was being treated for a heart condition."

He turned to Noguchi, who mysteriously sensed the fact and opened both eyes as Otani continued. "Right. Now we have three separate medical opinions as to the cause of death, even though it is probably safe to say that if the first pathologist had certified death by heart failure it would have gone unquestioned. I've already mentioned that we have independent evidence from the American doctor who was treating Liebermann that death could have occurred at any time. When I discussed this point with the District Prosecutor he was in some doubt about the implications of this. Anyway, it appears to have been established that Liebermann could not have committed suicide—at least not without assistance—but might have been murdered by a person of reasonable competence in judo."

"Especially if well known to Liebermann and on close personal terms with him," said Kimura, cutting in.

"Precisely," said Otani. "Finally—and I am still concerned with facts, not theories—we have apparently reliable evidence that the dead man was of bad character who might have been involved in dealing in pornographic photographs. Further, that he was in possession of an unregistered handgun which was new and unused and had been imported illegally into this country fairly recently. Now, Ninja—ah, Inspector Noguchi—I think you had better report on your visit to the firm's premises last night."

Noguchi heaved himself upwards in his chair by an inch or two, with an effect as great as a violent convulsion on the part of a lesser man. "Yes, well, I had two reasons for going last night. I wanted to do a bit of reconstruction with the help of this young fellow here. Confirmed that it could have been done by judo. Like you said. Also wanted to snoop around a bit. On the way to see the judo instructor Kimura mentioned the letters; one from Nakajima, straightforward business letter, he said. Wondered why he'd keep it in his pocket. Anyway, got through to Central Records. Computer says this Nakajima was convicted five years ago under the Gun Control Law.''

''*Was* he indeed?'' Otani's eyes were glittering as he turned to Migishima. ''You see, Constable, that a small amount of imagination can lead to a major piece of information!'' His gaze floated loftily over Kimura, who was sulking at being upstaged by Noguchi yet again, and returned to Noguchi.

''Splendid. So we now have solid grounds for presuming that Liebermann *was* smuggling guns. My word, we'd better organise a complete search of the warehouse right away . . .'' Otani's voice trailed off as he caught himself too late to avoid the inevitable.

Kimura was so mortified that his normal deft style in handling Otani was replaced by outrage. ''That's pure speculation! We were supposed to be talking about *facts*,'' he protested. ''Sir,'' he added rather weakly.

Otani shot an angry look at him and then spoke to Migishima. ''Inspector Kimura is right. Forget what I said for the moment. Note that the man who wrote to Liebermann had the conviction mentioned. We must call for a computer print-out of his arrest report. No doubt Inspector Kimura's section would have done this in due course anyway. Carry on, please, Ninja.''

The satisfaction Kimura felt at hearing what was clearly intended as a grudging acknowledgment of the justice of his intervention was very short-lived. Noguchi went on. ''Well, we were on our way up to the roof and out when someone came in below, took something from a drawer in the general office—key, it must have been—and went into the warehouse. Ten or fifteen minutes in there, and out again.'' He cocked an eyebrow at Migishima. ''That right, son?''

All three pairs of senior eyes turned to the young man who took a deep breath and replied firmly, addressing himself to Otani. ''Yes, sir. I was watching from cover. I noted the car number, and we checked it this morning.''

He paused, and Noguchi waved a hand irritably. "Go on. Tell the Superintendent the rest."

"Sir, the car had an Osaka registration. Mr Bunsho Maeda, sir. Inspector Noguchi thought he recognised him. I don't know about the lady. She didn't get out of the car."

Chapter 18

"**I** CAN'T BE OF VERY MUCH HELP IF YOU WON'T TELL me what's on your mind,'' said Akira Shimizu amiably enough. Otani still mooched along apparently aimlessly at his side. It was mid-afternoon, and the narrow alley lined with cheap eating-houses was quiet and gave the impression of a sleazy, down-at-heel whore half-heartedly making herself presentable and ready for the first punter of the evening.

Young men in singlets and jeans, their bare feet raised up on high wooden platform *geta* were sweeping and mopping the stone floors of the open-fronted bars and tidying up the high stools ranged inside. Behind, cooks were clattering beer-bottles and sharpening knives dulled by the lunchtime trade, and a few waitresses were gossiping among themselves during the slack period.

Otani could not have explained even to himself why, after closing the conference in his office, he had changed into his civilian clothes and told Tomita that he would not need the car for the rest of the day. He certainly wanted time to think, but it was an odd impulse that made him hail a taxi and go to the Shimizus' flat, where to his pleasure he found not only Akiko and the baby but also his son-in-law, in his oldest clothes, tidying up cracks in the walls with plastic filler. Akiko was very much less disposed than her mother to accept the conventions of the correct behaviour for a Japanese wife, and her protests had been lively and explicit when after a perfunctory inspection of his grandson and an even more token helping hand with the cracks Otani suggested that he and Shimizu might go and eat some *sushi* and drink some beer.

Nevertheless, something in her father's face cut her short, and by the time Shimizu had washed his hands and put on a different pair of trousers, her grumbles had become reasonably good-humoured. Shimizu was normally a good listener, but there had been precious little to listen to as Otani had moodily pointed to various kinds of fish in the refrigerated display and watched the *sushi* master deftly season the rice-cakes with a dab of tear-jerking *wasabi* paste before laying a slab of bream, a split prawn or slice of abalone on each of a neat pair.

It was not that Shimizu felt any kind of tension between the two of them; but for Otani to be so obviously forcing himself to make conversation was highly uncharacteristic, and made the odder by his earlier insistence that Shimizu should go out with him.

Otani now looked at him out of the corner of his eye. "Let's walk back by way of the zoo," he suggested.

Shimizu stopped in his tracks to engineer a minor confrontation. "Look," he said, "it wasn't easy to get leave from the office today, there's a lot to do at home, and I really ought to get back. But if it's important . . ."

Otani looked at him, then seemed to take himself in hand. "I'm sorry," he said. "I would like your advice, but I feel as though I shouldn't be bothering you. Walk on a bit more and I'll try to explain. If you hadn't told me all that about Liebermann I wouldn't have dreamed of discussing it again . . ." They walked on, and Shimizu kept completely silent as Otani gave him a neat and economical account of his own conversation with the Baron, and of the picture which had emerged during the morning conference (which Constable Migishima was at that moment summarising in a fractionally different way in his third re-draft of the report Otani had instructed him to have ready first thing next Monday morning).

At the end of the recital Shimizu still said nothing, but caught Otani's eye and raised both eyebrows interrogatively. "You want to know what we decided to do," said Otani. "Well, we've posted a guard on the warehouse, and I've sent Noguchi to Yokohama to look into the background of this man Nakajima. The computer records are easy enough to get, but there's no substitute for a talk with the local men."

"Are there that many convictions under the Gun Control Law?" Shimizu asked curiously. "I remember when I was running my protest faction at the university a couple of fairly tough characters contacted me to ask if we wanted any firearms. But we stuck to our trusty two-by-two wooden clubs."

"I know," said Otani reminiscently. "There's a fibreglass shield I used with the marks still on it somewhere . . . but to answer your question. It may surprise you that if you count firearm and sword control together as the law does, we get around four thousand convictions a year nationally. Nearly all gangsters, of course. And we confiscate something like fifteen hundred guns a year, believe it or not. Even so, there are rather a lot we don't find."

They were approaching the zoo gates, and Otani bought them each a bar of chocolate from the stall outside as Shimizu paid for the entrance tickets. Otani made straight for the monkey mountain and pointed out the wild boars wandering about its base, some of them with monkeys riding on their backs finding fleas. "The boars are the gangsters," he said. "The monkeys are the international contact men who keep them supplied with guns, drugs, European and American pornography and the rest of it. Ninja Noguchi's the man to look into the Yokohama end. There may be nothing in it, but if there is we shall go in tomorrow with a complete search team and have the lighter unloaded too.

"So far as the women are concerned, I've told Kimura to keep away from both of them for the moment. I want to have them in and question them myself."

"Are you going to the funeral?" asked Shimizu as they left the monkeys and drifted towards the cage containing the European sheep, always popular with the children. Otani shook his head. "I see very little point in it, and we shall probably have quite enough to do tomorrow as it is."

"That seems to leave Maeda and Dangoro. What about them?"

Otani sighed as he stared unseeingly at the peculiar creatures with their dirty woolly coats. "We shall have to have Dangoro in, though technically I ought to ask Osaka Police to handle it for me. Unless he happens to live in this Prefecture of course . . . we must look into that. Clearly he's on the edge of all this, even if he's not involved. I don't like to hound a man just because he's having a love affair. If that's all it is. Well, that leaves Maeda."

Otani turned and made for the gates, and Shimizu fell into step beside him, fascinated by the whole story but most of all by this particular twist in it. "It's not easy for me to think straight about him," Otani continued. "You know of course he was my chief at the end of the war. And ever since, he's been almost like a father to me. In fact he sponsored me for Rotary—no, don't laugh. It may seem ridiculous to you, but in that circle it's a very big thing."

He stopped as they negotiated the tall turnstile at the exit, and waited while Shimizu untangled the string of a hydrogen-filled balloon which a fat little boy had managed to get caught in the fence. "I hope you won't let Kazuo-chan get as fat as that child," he commented. "Do you know I read somewhere there are more obese children in Japan than in the whole of Europe?"

"Too many bean-jam buns and indulgent mothers," said Shimizu. "Can you see Akiko allowing that sort of thing? Anyway, go on about your aristocratic friend—no, I'm not being offensive, it's just that he looks the part so perfectly."

They walked back in the direction of the Shimizus' flat as Otani went on. "Well, in spite of the fact that it was becoming obvious that he's somehow mixed up in all this, I was dumbfounded when Noguchi said that he was pretty sure he recognised him even before the young officer noted the registration on the car. And then there's the woman sitting in it. Ninja got a good look at her, of course. Apparently she had a scarf over her head, but was definitely European. Well, it just has to be Mrs Liebermann."

He flung out his hands in an unusually extravagant gesture. "I *can't* delegate this to anybody. I've got to tax him with it myself. And what on earth do I do if he denies it? The Prosecutor will love me if I propose to charge him simply on the basis of the mishmash of rumour and speculation we have so far. And charge him with what? He didn't break in and according to my people he didn't even act furtively."

"He must have said something when Noguchi claimed to be the night watchman from the next wharf," said Shimizu.

"Yes, but it doesn't help me much," Otani replied. "He just told him he was checking on the security of the premises. Didn't identify himself in any way, but behaved as though he owned the place, Noguchi said. Then gave him five thousand yen for his trouble and asked him to keep an eye on things till all the earthquake damage repairs were finished."

"What do you think the old man could be up to, then?" Shimizu slowed down as they neared the flats, and Otani stopped altogether.

"I wish I could begin to guess," he said. "He told me himself he knew Mrs Liebermann; and obviously knows all the puppeteers. He said he knew Liebermann quite well, and practically in as many words asked me to accept the heart attack theory and drop the case. That could only be to protect somebody: and I'm sick to think it must be the murderer."

He looked at his watch. "I must be getting back. Hanae will be wondering where I am. Thanks, Akira." He hardly ever used the young man's name, and Shimizu looked at him curiously.

"You said you wanted my advice," he said. "You haven't asked for it, and I haven't given any."

Otani smiled briefly. "On the contrary, you've been very helpful," he said. "I needed to think aloud, and I needed the questions you asked. The trouble with Kimura and Noguchi is that they tend to go off on their own tracks and leave me at the station. At least the Baron is my responsibility, and I know what to do next."

He gave a little farewell wave and turned away, but Shimizu stopped him. "Well, what are you going to do?"

Otani looked at him. "I'm going to go and see him," he said. "Now I really must be going. Give Akiko my love and tell her I'm sorry I stole you. Oh, and I promise to tell you what happens."

"So I should hope," said Shimizu severely, then waved his arm as he saw a taxi in the distance. "Take care of yourself."

Chapter 19

"**Y**OU ARE VERY MUCH MORE EFFICIENT THAN I EVER dreamed, Otani-san. Do not misunderstand me, I have always had the highest opinion of your abilities. But I am completely at a loss to know how you came by this information. I was assured that the police had completed all their enquiries at the Hochmuth-Wassermann premises the previous day."

"Assured by whom?" The two men were in the exquisite garden of the Baron's old-fashioned house not a great distance from Otani's own. The afternoon sun was still high and bright, and the air was thickening into its summer heat. They were standing at the edge of the ornamental pool feeding the huge multicoloured carp which flocked to them and whose round gaping mouths broke the surface in their efforts to reach the pieces of breadstick which Otani and the Baron were breaking off and tossing into the water.

"By the chief accountant there—what's his name, Sato or Sakai or something like that. I telephoned to express condolences on behalf of the Chamber of Commerce and to ask about the funeral arrangements. He told me they were in the hands of the German Consulate General."

Otani sighed yet again. It had been painful to telephone Maeda and propose the visit without mentioning its purpose, and to hear him agree so readily. It had been even more painful to go through the courteous preliminaries of green tea and little cakes served by the old countrywoman from the former Maeda estates who had once been one of a whole platoon of servants and who now took care of him with the help of one young girl and a gardener.

It was something to be down to reasonably straight talking, and after the initial look of utter astonishment when Otani had asked him to say whether or not he had been at the Hochmuth-Wassermann warehouse on the previous evening, the Baron had soon recovered his habitual bland manner.

"Frankly speaking, our enquiries are very far from complete," Otani said. "And I much regret that I must ask you a great many questions. It would be helpful if you would be willing to explain why you were at the warehouse, and confirm that the lady with you was Mrs Liebermann. I hope so much that it will not be necessary for me to subject you to a formal interrogation. Much will depend on how much you are willing to volunteer."

The old man was wearing a *yukata* and wooden *geta*, and he straightened the hem of the *yukata* before stepping a little nearer to the water. "*There*, my beauty," he murmured, pitching a piece of bread directly to a smaller but beautiful fish with iridescent red-gold markings. "Isn't he splendid, Otani-san? But then he should be, I paid five hundred thousand for him from the breeder." Otani remained silent, and after a while the Baron looked at him quizzically.

"Very well, Otani-san. I will tell you why I was with Mrs Liebermann. It was her, of course. After you told me at Rotary that you were trying to find her I made my own enquiries and telephoned the house several times. There was no reply until very late that night, and I had a long talk with her, knowing that she would be greatly distressed. I tried to break the news to her that there was a doubt about her husband's death, but she already knew about your investigations. Shall we go and see if the azalea are likely to come into bloom soon?"

The Baron's measured tones drifted back to Otani as he followed him along the stepping stones placed across one end of the pond, the palest mauve of the irises soft against the moss of the bank. "I fear, you see, that Liebermann was not the respectable businessman he seemed. That is to say, he was not *only* the respectable etcetera. Mrs Liebermann has been living with a very unpleasant secret, Otani-san."

They reached the neatly trimmed azalea bushes on the far side of the pond, and the old man scrutinised them with care. "Another couple of weeks, I should say, wouldn't you?"

"About that," Otani agreed patiently, giving him the time to think he so obviously wanted.

"Yes," said the Baron, straightening up. "A very disagreeable business. I suppose it will all have to come out anyway, so it is better you should have it from me. Let us sit down on those stones over there."

They made their way to two magnificent boulders which must have cost a fortune, naturally shaped as they were to provide comfortable seats, and when they were settled, Maeda continued without interrupting himself further. "I told you that I met Irmgard Liebermann about a year ago, and then heard of her friendship with Dangoro through my connection with the *bunraku* company. That was not strictly accurate. As a matter of fact, I met her in Dangoro's company first, and came to know and like her very much."

He stretched out a thin hand and rested it on the warm stone. "I found it odd that Liebermann seemed positively to encourage her in her relationship and one day I gently raised the question with her. I was very surprised by the bitterness of her reaction, and formed the opinion that Liebermann was mistreating her in some way. It was not until much later that she confided in Dangoro, and worried him so much that he came to consult me."

Otani opened his mouth to speak, and Maeda raised his hand from the boulder to stop him. "Yes, yes," he said a little testily. "I will tell you why he consulted me. You will find out sooner or later and I am too old to worry about it. He is my son. His mother was a *geisha* in Tokyo. She was killed in an air-raid when he was a small boy, and I arranged to have him looked after in the country; but that is all by the way. We are concerned with Liebermann."

The Baron rubbed his eyes and then looked directly at Otani. "And now I am confiding in you. Well, to be brief, Liebermann *did* speak excellent Japanese. He learned during the war, as I hinted to you the other day. He was here as a junior member of a military liaison mission, and seems to have managed to retain a few links over all those years. I have no idea whether he revisited this country before being sent here by his firm. He may have done. At all events, he nosed about to some purpose once he was established here in Kobe. I don't know whether you yourself have been much concerned with the links between the gangs and large-scale business, Otani-san?"

Otani shook his head. "A humble prefectural policeman doesn't do much in that line," he said, feeling almost relaxed as the story seemed to be tumbling out. "The Criminal Investigation Bureau of the National Police Agency plays in that game."

"Well," said Maeda tranquilly, "let me instruct you a little. One of the ways in which the gangs obtain payoffs from legitimate business is by permeating and then acquiring subsidiary firms, then letting the parent company know the price they require to refrain from disturbing shareholders' annual general meetings. It results in a very confused and unclear dividing line between the legitimate and the illegitimate."

He smiled wryly at Otani. "How much simpler it was in the old days when it was just a matter of fighting for the Greater Japanese Empire," he said. "Let me go on. Liebermann in his legitimate capacity was under contract to supply bearings to a firm of heavy mechanical engineers which was part of a much bigger conglomerate but which in turn was supplied by a number of smaller manufacturing companies, one at least of which was completely controlled by a gang operating in the Yokohama area. In addition to the bearings Liebermann also supplied firearms. Everything came from Germany; and his suppliers there organised the amalgamation of the shipments with the consignments of genuine bearings. They also made sure that the shipping documents were all in order. Are you following me?"

174

Otani nodded hesitantly. "I think so, but how do you know all this?"

Maeda smiled again. "I'm getting rather old, and rather tired," he said, "but I made quite a lot of money in business and you can't do that just by being an ex-aristocrat." There was more than a touch of pride in his expression. "I was perfectly able to piece the puzzle together once I had an inkling, and found he was in touch with people in certain companies." He reached out and patted Otani's knee. "Don't be anxious about that excellent young fellow Shimizu," he said hastily. "I can assure you that his reputation could not be higher, and justly.

"Neither Dangoro nor I could understand why Irmgard kept returning to Liebermann. My son pointed out to her that she was contributing to his criminal activities merely by keeping silent. All she would do was burst into tears and say that with his bad heart he would surely die soon and she would be free. Then we discovered that Liebermann was tormenting his wife. He was a beastly man, you know; a foul sadistic creature." The old man shivered in the warm sunshine, and Otani looked at him curiously.

"Yes," he said. "I'd begun to gather that."

"I'll continue, Otani-san," said the Baron, his thin hands again motionless on the blue and white material of the *yukata*. "It must all come out. Dangoro went to see Liebermann just before the holidays to plead with him to divorce Irmgard since she seemed unable or unwilling to initiate anything herself. And . . . I understand that Liebermann taunted him. He said that Irmgard was essential to his business dealings, and that he had excellent reasons to know that she would continue to collaborate with him. Then he asked Dangoro whether he wanted to know why, and without waiting for an answer said he would send him copies of the pictures anyway. That it would amuse him to think that Dangoro knew what Irmgard would rather die than have him find out."

The Baron's lean, chiselled face looked taut and drawn. "I've almost finished," he said quietly. "A day or two later an envelope was delivered to . . . my son . . . at the theatre. It contained three photographs of Irmgard, being . . . being

175

outraged by Liebermann's dog. The poor woman was obviously only half-conscious; drugged or drunk, I couldn't say.'' He stopped speaking, and looked absently round the garden. ''Dangoro was almost insane with anger,'' he said after a while. ''I persuaded him not to be foolish. To tell you the truth, Otani-san, I told him that I would take certain steps myself . . . it is not all that difficult for a man in my position to arrange for delicate tasks to be carried out.''

He looked Otani straight in the face and smiled with singular sweetness. ''How fortunate it was that Liebermann had a heart attack on Boys' Day,'' he said softly. ''I'm sure he did, you know.''

Otani looked at him sadly. ''I wish so much that it were so,'' he said. ''I am grateful to you from my heart for speaking to me as you have, and I wish I could close the case. You must give me a little time to think about all this. One question you still haven't answered, though: why did you go to the warehouse?''

The Baron stood up and stretched himself delicately. ''Irmgard knows the code numbers used on the crates containing the 'special shipments'. She wanted to know if there were any in the warehouse. She was afraid of what might come out of a police search, and now of course there will surely be one.''

Otani stood as well, and they began to move slowly back to the house. ''Will we find anything?'' he asked.

Maeda nodded. ''You would if you were to look,'' he said, ''but I think you might be better advised to follow the consignment to its destination and arrange to be there when it is opened by the people who ordered it.''

Chapter 20

Hanae found Otani impossible for the rest of the day, and he was still impossible the next morning. He barely touched his breakfast, and snapped at her when she tried to persuade him to eat. Tomita came with the car while Otani was still upstairs, and she went out to chat to him for a minute or two as she sometimes did. When Otani finally stumped out of the house Hanae turned to him with a bright smile.

"Tomita-san has been telling me all about the dog. Kimura-san found out what his name is and Tomita-san's been teaching him tricks . . ." Her voice trailed off in amazement as Otani's face darkened with anger.

"If you say one more word about that animal I'll have you transferred!" he stormed at Tomita, then turned to Hanae and seemed to be about to rage at her too. Then he closed his mouth, opened it again and closed it for a second time. "I'm sorry," he said curtly. "I'll see you later."

Hanae bowed sadly as he climbed stiffly into the car and stared grimly ahead as it rolled forward. She couldn't imagine what had got into Otani after a visit to the Baron of the kind he normally enjoyed so much, and wondered if she would ever find out.

Otani for his part tried to marshal his unruly thoughts as

177

the car moved down the hilly roads towards the main highway and he gazed glumly at the back of Tomita's neck, stiff as it was with injured innocence. Eventually he brought himself to apologise. "I am sorry I spoke to you in that way, Tomita," he said gruffly. "I'm not feeling very well today." Tomita was immediately all conciliatory concern, and Otani had to discourage him from driving him at once to the hospital. "No no, it's quite all right. All the same, I'd rather you didn't speak about the dog. I'm sure you'll be able to keep it if you wish, by the way." This so pleased Tomita that from his point of view normal relations were completely restored, and he left Otani to his thoughts.

The first thing to be done was obviously to see what Noguchi had managed to dig up from Yokohama Police, and then let him concentrate on following up the information about Liebermann's gun-smuggling activities without alerting anyone along the chain of communication. A very good thing that their half-formulated plan to stage a full-scale raid on the Hochmuth-Wassermann warehouse had as yet been taken no further. The investigation group at the National Police Agency would be much better pleased to have the whole bag of information dumped neatly into their laps to handle as they saw fit.

Then the Liebermann woman would obviously have to be seen. Better perhaps to keep Kimura out of it, even if it would hurt his feelings: he seemed to have got into quite deep enough water with the other one, the secretary. Of course, Irmgard Liebermann might want to have a representative of her Consulate present. Still, that would be a privilege, not a right. A preliminary informal chat, perhaps, then she might not insist on using German, which would rule Kimura out conveniently but would be awkward all the same.

The car pulled up outside Headquarters and Tomita shot out and opened Otani's door, making solicitous gestures of assistance as though Otani were in an advanced stage of some mortal illness rather than having mentioned being off-colour. Brushing him off, Otani made his way up to his office to find Migishima prowling in the corridor nervously.

"Sir. Good morning, sir. A lady to see you, sir. A foreign lady, sir," he stuttered.

Otani stopped and surveyed him coldly. "Did Inspector Kimura refer her to me?"

Migishima shook his head. "No, sir. The duty officer took a call last night from the lady asking for an appointment early today. It's Mrs Liebermann, sir. Particularly insistent that she would speak to you personally and in confidence. Particularly said she did not wish to speak to any other senior officer. She was told the request would be put to you first thing today, and asked what time that would be. They told her not before nine o'clock. She was here waiting when I arrived at eight-thirty. Sir."

Otani opened his mouth to reprimand Migishima for bringing her upstairs, then thought better of it. Perhaps it was just as well that Kimura had been by-passed. Mrs Liebermann must have something pressing on her mind if she wanted to see him on the morning of the day her husband's ashes were to be buried among those of the other foreigners in the special cemetery at Futatabi.

"Have you spoken to her yourself, Migishima?" he asked.

"Just to escort her up here, sir. I wasn't sure what you would wish, sir. She seemed very anxious to wait for you in private."

Otani nodded. "I think you did the right thing," he said. "How good is her Japanese?"

"Oh, very good, sir," Migishima replied, blushing. "I tried to use a few words of German but she answered me so fluently in Japanese that I was ashamed."

Otani stretched out a hand towards the handle of his door, then withdrew it. It was excellent that she had turned up, but he would have very much liked more time to think about the best way to handle the interview. Kimura was a nuisance but his easy way with foreigners made him a distinctly comforting presence when they had to be questioned, quite apart from his flair for languages. At all events, the last thing he wanted was Migishima blundering about trying to be helpful.

"Very well," he said. "I'll go in and see her. If and only

179

if I buzz for you, come in and we'll offer her some refreshment. Have you any instant coffee in there?''

Migishima nodded dubiously. ''I think so, sir. It's gone a bit hard in the jar but I think I could use it.''

''All right. But don't do anything unless I buzz. Is that understood? While I'm talking to her ring Inspector Kimura and tell him I'm in private conference and would like to see him . . . but that you'll let him know. Ah, if he asks you, you are to say that you don't know who I have with me.''

Feeling slightly ashamed of his duplicity, Otani nodded curtly at Migishima, opened his door and went into his room. He had hardly ever met European women socially, but had noticed in films their curiously ill-mannered custom of remaining seated when being introduced to a man. Fortunately, Mrs Liebermann's behaviour was impeccable. She rose immediately from the easy chair in which she had been sitting, bowed to him gracefully and murmured exactly the right courteous apologies in extremely polite Japanese. (Much later Otani told Hanae that his immediate reaction was to wish that the younger generation of Japanese women were half so mannerly.)

''There can be no excuse for my intruding upon the Superintendent in this abrupt fashion,'' she said humbly.

''Not at all,'' Otani replied in the appropriate vein. ''I am honoured by your visit to this uncomfortable office. Allow me to introduce myself: I am called Otani. Please extend your favour to me.'' They continued bowing to each other as she took up the dialogue.

''I am Liebermann. It is the first time we have met. I apologise for interrupting you when I am sure you are very busy.''

Otani straightened up and made hospitable gestures. ''Please sit down. I expect you find this warm weather troublesome. May I offer you some green tea?''

The words slipped out before he remembered the plans he had laid with Migishima for the provision of coffee, but this lady seemed so comfortably Japanese to Otani that green tea was the obvious thing. Mrs Liebermann politely demurred twice and then allowed herself to be persuaded, and Otani pressed the buzzer to summon Migishima, who became confused by his instructions and after a few minutes brought two cups each of green tea and instant coffee, to be on the safe side.

Only then did Otani allow himself to offer formal condolences to the widow and express the mildest possible gratification that she had found it possible to call on him on the very day of the funeral. Mrs Liebermann remained composed, but Otani saw her mouth tighten, and she smoothed her black skirt over her knees before she too began to approach the central substance of the conversation.

"You have been most kind to agree to see me this morning," she began; and Otani forbore to point out that he had in any case intended to summon her before long. "As you know, my late husband's funeral is to be this afternoon, and I would like to answer any questions you may have for me before that."

Otani nodded thoughtfully. "Your coming here is much appreciated, Mrs Liebermann. It is a matter of much regret that I have to put questions to you at all at such an unhappy time; but you will have been informed by your Consul that there is unfortunately a doubt about the circumstances of your husband's death." He sucked in air through his teeth to give himself time to phrase his next remarks. "Ah . . . perhaps, so as not to waste your valuable time, I might ask why you particularly wish to deal with the matter this morning?"

Mrs Liebermann seemed to gather her forces within her to a focus; a kind of clenching of the spirit like a Zen master about to give expression with his ink-brush to the concept of a poem. When she spoke it was simply and to the point. "I know nothing about my husband's death being hastened. He was in any case very near to death. I know that you spoke to Maeda-san yesterday, and something of what he told you. You are aware of my relationship with Dangoro. I had at one time thought it might be possible to remain in Japan. Now he and I wish to leave this country and make a new life together in Europe, in Germany. We wish to go very soon, and I wish to receive your permission to do so."

In the long silence which followed, she seemed to slacken all over and almost slump in her chair, and Otani had a momentary vision of her as one of Dangoro's puppets, a rag doll until the life flowed into her from him. He then felt an overwhelming sadness as he recalled the look in the Baron's eyes as they had sat on the warm boulders in his tranquil garden, and wished profoundly that he could turn back the clock. Why had he taken it into his head to go for a drive round the wharves? Why had he heard the dog, officiously barged in, and then felt so proud of himself for not accepting the obvious?

After a long time Otani spoke gently and quietly. "You have spoken with sincerity, and I am grateful. I will now speak to you personally, and not as a police official. I can only say this. I now know that you have no reason to mourn Richard Liebermann. I also know—and this may perhaps surprise you—that Dangoro loves you greatly, perhaps more than you can understand, and that Maeda-san is your friend. Now, as a policeman, I must say that all three of you—Dangoro, Maeda and you yourself—are under suspicion. I *cannot*, much as I might wish, give you permission to leave Japan until my investigation is complete."

He sighed and tried to smile. "I am confident that this will be soon; and I will personally ensure that as soon as the way is clear you will be authorised to leave. In the meantime, we shall try not to distress you further; but I must ask you to arrange for your Consul to know where we can make contact with you at all times. Please don't take this amiss—we shall require the same of Dangoro and of . . . the Baron."

He stood and after a few seconds Irmgard Liebermann also rose. Her bow was less perfect this time, and Otani looked away as he saw tears in her fine eyes. He went to the desk and buzzed for Migishima, who came in at once and stood stiffly to attention. "You will escort Mrs Liebermann to the main entrance and instruct my driver that he is to take her in my car wherever she wishes to go," he said stiffly.

"Please . . . that will not be necessary," she whispered, fumbling in her handbag and finding a tissue.

"Please. I should like to help you if I possibly can," Otani said, and moved to the door. She went out slowly, and he bowed again as she passed. Otani watched Migishima lead her down the corridor with clumsy solicitude, and then found it necessary to blow his own nose.

Chapter 21

"**B**UT THIS IS RIDICULOUS!" OTANI LOOKED INCREDulously from one sheet of paper to the other as Kimura danced about excitedly in front of his desk. "It's not possible. Keep *still*, man!"

Kimura took a pace or two away, then wheeled round, and snapped the fingers of both hands together. "Chief, it all fits in, don't you see?"

Otani shook his head dubiously and peered again at the two documents before him. "A photocopy of a photograph is hopeless," he grumbled. "Yes, they're much of an age, and there's a slight resemblance, I suppose . . ."

"They're the *same person*," Kimura insisted. "I know it, Chief. I know I only saw the back of her head as your car pulled away, but I got Migishima to describe her. I'll swear it was Ilse Fischer. Look, just let me go to the funeral, that's all. Then if I'm wrong I'll apologise."

Otani managed a brief smile. "You? That's hardly likely." He got up himself and went over to the window. "How in the world could she have kept it up? For two whole years?"

Kimura sensed that he was beginning to entertain the possibility, and strove to be both eloquent and controlled. "Entry on false papers. By no means impossible. If Liebermann was part of an international gun-running chain he could easily persuade the people at the German end of the advantages of having his own wife placed as his secretary in the firm. The two of them could cope with all the illicit side of the business and let the Japanese staff deal with the legitimate imports.'' He paused to think of flaws.

"They would probably need accomplices in the actual warehouse—we'll need to look into that. The Yokohama end could easily have fixed that up. Right. Well, crooked gun-dealers aren't likely to have any trouble arranging a little matter like a false passport in the name of Ilse Fischer. Mrs Liebermann goes home to Germany for a holiday two years ago—we can check that—and comes back as Miss Fischer, who very conveniently goes to stay with the Liebermanns until she finds a place of her own.''

Kimura smote his forehead in a theatrical manner. "I thought it was peculiar. Apart from a weird collection of toys the flat seemed very empty. Not many clothes, nothing lying about as you'd expect. And it wasn't as if she'd expected a visitor and tidied up specially. Then, you see, Chief, she told me she turned down the invitations that came her way and in effect disappeared so far as the foreign community were concerned. They forget people pretty quickly, there's so many changes among them all the time.''

"What about Dangoro?'' said Otani, still looking out of the window. "How could she have handled that meeting you told me about?''

Kimura reflected, trying to recall exactly what was said. Dangoro had certainly used the name Ilse, but had been speaking English at the time. "I'm not completely sure,'' he admitted. "Certainly they were on very relaxed terms. She spoke to him for a long time in German, and could have been filling him in on the whole thing so far as I know.''

Otani turned round and went back to his desk for another look at the foreigners' registration sheets from Kimura's files. "I blame myself for not comparing them sooner,'' said Kimura with a transparently insincere show of humility.

"No reason why you should," Otani grunted absently, then looked up. "Well, it's still incredible to me, but I must say it would answer some difficult questions." He took his glasses off and played with them. "Dangoro must have known—if all this is true," he added hastily. "So must Maeda. Well, Kimura, you'd better go to this funeral and have another look at her. You'll feel a bit of a fool if they both turn up. In the meantime . . ."

He was interrupted in mid-sentence as the door was flung open and Migishima came in. With a sidelong glance at Kimura he went over to Otani and tried to whisper in his ear. Otani drew back irritably. "What do you mean by bursting in like this, Constable?" His brusqueness faded as the import of the young man's words sank in. "Are you sure? She hung up?" Migishima nodded and Otani scrambled to his feet. "Is Tomita back yet?"

Migishima nodded again. "Yes, sir. He rang from the garage about twenty minutes ago. Mrs Liebermann went home, sir."

Otani looked at Kimura, whose look of triumphant self-satisfaction had been replaced by one of concern. "I must go home, Kimura," he said. "My wife just telephoned to say I'm needed. I don't know what it is, but it seems she sounded upset." He hesitated, anxiety about Hanae chasing the ferment of ideas triggered off by Kimura's astonishing theory. "Stay here till lunchtime at least, and I'll telephone. Don't mention this idea of yours to anyone else just yet." He turned to Migishima. "My car. Main entrance, immediately."

Migishima was already speaking into the telephone as Otani swept out of the room, and Otani had to wait only for two impatient minutes before Tomita brought the car round. "No, I'm quite all right, Tomita," he snapped in response to further enquiries about his health. "Home please, and get a move on."

Otani sat back and drummed his fingers nervously on his knee as Tomita negotiated the heavy mid-morning traffic with his habitual careful skill. It was almost unheard of for Hanae to ring him at his office; and for her to betray distress so obviously that it bothered Migishima was deeply troubling.

Perhaps some accident had befallen little Kazuo, or Akiko. "Can't you make any better time?" he demanded, and Tomita shook his head.

"Very heavy traffic, sir." Something in Otani snapped.

"Put the siren on," he said.

After a moment's incredulity, Tomita did so, and the car surged forward as others gave way to the wailing of the siren and the flashing light which Tomita had never used previously with the Superintendent on board. The gods be praised that it was all in working order. Less than ten minutes later they were sweeping up the hilly roads towards the house, and Otani told Tomita to switch it off again.

Otani made a good deal of noise as he rattled the sliding door open, and in any case shouted his usual "I'm home!" Hanae didn't answer at once, or with her customary response, and it was not until Otani had kicked off his shoes and was mounting the polished wooden step that he heard a small voice and the words "I'm upstairs."

Convinced that she must be ill, Otani flung himself up the stairs, his heart pounding, to find Hanae fully dressed and kneeling with her head bowed before the flower arrangement in the alcove in the reception room in which they also slept. "What is it? Are you ill? What's happened?" The words tumbled out as he sank to his knees beside her.

Hanae turned a tear-stained face towards him and said nothing, but indicated two poems on beautiful edged paper lying in the alcove. Otani snatched them up and peered at them. The calligraphy was bold and free; the brushstrokes serenely right. He blinked at them uncomprehendingly. *Haiku* had never been his strong suit, and although he could see the beauty with his eyes, the meanings eluded him. He focused on the red impression of the seal of the writer. Maeda. Maeda. A sick lurching began in his stomach as Hanae took the papers from him gently.

"They were delivered about half an hour ago," she said falteringly. "In one envelope, addressed to both of us. Mine is the one I recognise—by Taigi I think." She held the paper out and read it aloud.

> In the late autumn
> Look! Morning glory springs up
> From my rubbish-dump

"I wondered what could be the meaning," Hanae said. "At first I was happy. Something beautiful towards the end of his life. Then I read yours." Her face crumpled and she could hardly finish even the short seventeen syllables.

> When they ask for me
> Tell them I had some business
> In another world

Otani had to stop himself from running out of the house like a madman and bellowing for Tomita before realising how much more important it was to comfort Hanae.

It was half an hour later that the car drew up quietly outside the high outer gate of the Maeda mansion which he had approached on foot in casual clothes only twenty-four hours before. The old housekeeper was surprised to see him again. "I think that the Baron is in the garden with his fish," she said.

He looked quite peaceful when Otani found him lying on the moss at the edge of the pond, his wrists in the water, and for a moment he thought he must be sleeping. The old man had not needed to lose much blood, which was good. He would not have wanted to disturb the carp too much. Otani sat in the warm sun beside him for a long time, his mind ranging over more than half his lifetime. Then he very slowly got up and went to tell the old housekeeper to remain with the maid in the kitchen. The gardener was nowhere to be seen anyway, but the Baron weighed very little and Otani was able to carry him like a child to the house, bind up the thin wrists and lay him in dignity on the soft golden tatami mats of the finest room.

Then he went to the telephone and spoke to Kimura.

Chapter 22

"**W**ELL, DID THEY GET OFF SAFELY?" ASKED OTANI as Kimura walked in, natty in what was evidently yet another new outfit. Kimura nodded and made for the easy chairs in response to Otani's gesture, remaining standing until Otani had settled himself and heaved a satisfied sigh.

"I went right through to the departure lounge, courtesy of the Immigration and Customs people. Had quite a long talk to them both before they boarded, and then watched them take off. They'll be in Hong Kong in a couple of hours from now, then on to Germany."

Otani reached into his jacket pocket and pulled out a packet of Hope cigarettes. He offered it to Kimura who took one and glanced at the English wording on the packet. "Appropriate," he said. Otani looked at him enquiringly. Like most Japanese he had never bothered to wonder why the Japan tobacco monopoly corporation labelled their products in an alien language, and had no idea what the brand name signified. Kimura translated, and then went on to explain until Otani cut him short.

"Yes, I take the point," he said amiably enough. "Well, I hope so too. What she told us in her statement was useful enough for me to be able to persuade the District Prosecutor

189

to agree to simple deportation on the false immigration declaration charge.''

Kimura nodded. ''Yes. And she knows she'll have some explaining to do to the German police. Still, Interpol know the value of an inside informant.''

Otani puffed at his cigarette and stared up at the freshly painted ceiling. ''Ninja's having the time of his life,'' he said thoughtfully. ''The Agency loves us, and we've confiscated enough firearms to re-equip the entire Prefectural force. Well, it's almost over now. The Prosecutor agreed to accept Maeda's suicide as confirmation of his oral statement to me. So the file's closed.''

Otani showed no signs of anxiety to get rid of him, and Kimura was emboldened to try to draw him out. ''He died in a good samurai spirit,'' he said tentatively.

Otani smiled reflectively. ''He was a sort of samurai all the years I knew him,'' he said. ''Though I don't know what kind of a lord he would have made in the middle ages. His family had become rather flabby, till he redeemed it during the war. He was a good, straight commander; and I think I can understand how he managed to become so successful in business. How his ancestors would have disapproved of that!''

''I'm glad we made no difficulty over letting Dangoro have a passport to leave,'' said Kimura. ''He was quite chatty at the airport. Needless to say, Ilse had told him who I really was.'' He stubbed out his cigarette with an air of embarrassment.

''Of course, I now realise that she was just very clumsily trying to divert me from realising how attached she was to him. It all helped to build up the separate character in my mind.''

Otani raised an eyebrow. ''What on earth are you talking about?'' he enquired. Kimura looked away.

''Well, there was a moment when I thought she might have taken a fancy to me,'' he muttered.

Otani looked at him with a weary smile. ''Kimura-kun, Kimura-kun. You're hopeless. How would you like me to find you a wife?''

Kimura looked up in momentary horror, then smiled in his turn. "Sorry, I thought for a moment you meant it," he said. "We were talking about Maeda at the airport. I thought there was no longer any point in beating about the bush, so I asked them why they thought he'd left the dog there instead of turning it loose. Ilse really hated that dog, you know. Strange really."

"I don't know that it is," said Otani quietly. "What did they say?"

"Well, she just looked upset and I felt embarrassed at having mentioned it. I said something about Tomita being so happy to have him, and then Dangoro said it was just as well you'd come along when you did, because the food in the bowl had most likely been poisoned. Then the plane was called, and that was the last I saw of them." Kimura began to get up and Otani made no move to stop him.

With the door half open, Kimura turned back. "Migishima's delighted, sir," he said.

"I know," said Otani. "It's only for six months, mind. Then he must be transferred to get wider experience. I had thought he might go to your section. You could use some help with German, Kimura." Kimura opened his mouth and then shut it again as he so often did with Otani, who went on speaking.

"By the way, Kimura, you mustn't assume that because the Baron implied he killed Liebermann he really did," he said tranquilly. "You pointed out that a woman could have done it, but an old man in his seventies?" He leaned back and yawned. "Do you know how much a *bunraku* puppet weighs? Something like fifteen kilos. If you hold one of those things up for several hours a day you develop extraordinarily powerful forearms. I'll see you tomorrow."

Otani looked at his watch and decided to go home early. Hanae would understand if he had a little whisky that night.

About the Author

JAMES MELVILLE was born in London in 1931 and educated in North London. He read philosophy at Birkbeck College before being conscripted into the RAF, then took up school-teaching and adult education. Most of his subsequent career has been spent overseas in cultural diplomacy and educational development, and it was in this capacity that he came to know, love, and write about Japan and the Japanese. He has two sons and is married to a singer-actress. He continues to write more mystery novels starring Superintendent Otani.

CO**N**SPIRACY

MU**R**DER

INTRIGUE *From* **Fawcett Books**